GERAINT
the
REBEL'S SON

CHARL VISBY

Published in Great Britain 2018 by Frederick Charles Davies

ISBN 978-1-9996482-0-6

Printed by CreateSpace

Proof Reader Julie Rushton
Designer Claire Steele
Typeset in Bembo and Stonecross.
Images from www.shutterstock.com
and www.pixabay.com

Dedicated to my dear daughter Jo Poole and her husband Dave with gratitude and thanks for everything. Also to Roger and Julie Rushton for their loyal and continuous support at all times.

Produced with gratitude to God for granting my darling wife Jean and myself some fifty-eight wonderful married years.

CHAPTER
I

Geraint Cadwaladr screamed. His yell carried along the Welsh mountainside. Thrusting himself into the copious fronds he buried his face in his arms; his hands thrashed the ground. Weeping intensely, his little body shook. Having just witnessed his father Hywel's horrendous slaughter, he thumped the ground harder and with all the spite he could muster swore he'd kill that murderous Roman centurion when he was older.

Eight-year-old Geraint's life had been suddenly shattered. Having wholly idolised his father he then had nobody to care for him and love him. Two years earlier their hut had been set alight by the Romans: his dear mother and two siblings had been burned to death. That tragic day he'd been secretly following his father as he often did, when he'd witnessed that dreadful event. The boy's hatred for the intruding foreigners which had been strongly associated with that of his father was instantly increased.

Hywel's detestation of the Romans had long been pronounced. Having desperately wanted to eject them from his beloved Cymru he'd entered one of the tribal chief Mawddach's huts to demand positive action from his brother. As usual, his son had been with him, for he completely doted on his sole remaining child who was always beside him except when Hywel was at war. Even then the boy, out of mischief, frequently trailed behind at an unseen distance.

Mawddach proved as resolute and domineering as ever. He stated emphatically that he wouldn't tolerate uniting with the neighbouring Deceanglis and immediately flew into a rage. They were the main source of his many hatreds. "Not ruling this tribe, you are!" he screamed. "No association with that murderous Berwyn Goch ever we will have, so that to do, don't tell me!" For years, the two tribes had fiercely fought each other and the animosity between the leaders had positively increased. "No right a suggestion like that to make, you have!" he screamed savagely. The wolfhound which he kept close by growled menacingly at its master's noise. "Down, lie!" bawled its owner attempting to kick at it. The dog withdrew, showing its teeth, as Mawddach turned away.

His brother's reaction didn't altogether surprise Hywel but his affection for his beloved country was far too great to accept his decision. He became determined to defy the directive whatever the cost. "Too stupidly opposed to the Deceanglis to agree, you are!" he stated firmly. "Better to unite with fellow Celts, no matter what you think of them than let these perishing Romans infiltrate into our land and all this trouble cause us."

"Like that don't you dare talk to me!" snapped the chief. "Me to rule this tribe it is, not you!" He displayed his left shoulder which had the image of a crow holding a twig in its mouth. "Gives me complete authority that does – over you too – so don't you ever forget it!" he yelled. Once more the dog rose and issued another vicious growl. "Down lie!" Mawddach screamed again as his foot shot out once more. The animal obeyed, baring its teeth.

"Not fit our ruler to be you are when these foreigners trample our beloved land you let!"

Mawddach swiped at him with his very heavy stick; Hywel only just avoided being struck. Geraint had instinctively started to move to protect his father, his small fists tightly clenched, but he checked himself and pulled back as the wolfhound snarled at him with exposed teeth.

"Lucky my brother you are, or pegged to the ground and left to die for that you would be! Only that crow without a branch has saved you." There was no doubt that the elder sibling would have been delighted to have had him tethered to the ground. The lack of relationship between them was intense but as Hywel was very popular and respected within the tribe, Mawddach feared any such action against his brother would have caused so much unrest that he couldn't have tolerated it. "Out, get!" he ordered,

"Before you and this horrible child I thrash!"

On leaving Mawddach they came across Hywel's young friend Iorwerth Morgwn. "Rather sad you look, Hywel. Something the matter, is there?"

Hywel related in detail what had transpired with Mawddach, and Iorwerth expressed total sympathy. "Yes, wrong he is. Something to stop these Romans must be done or trample all over us they will. Still, almost impossible to make arrangements with that dreadful Berwyn Goch it will be. Just as stupid and vicious as our leader he is. Not to be trusted at all!"

"Fully understand that I do, but try something we must or completely overtake us they will!"

"Yes, but how about it will you go?" He sounded worried.

"That I don't yet know. Think very much about it and developments wait for, I'll have to."

For days Hywel had cautiously trespassed into Deceangli territory to see if he could find Berwyn in an acceptable situation: he carried his club as a precaution. He'd excitedly hoped to meet up with that brutal leader despite it being such a great risk. Unbeknown to him though he'd been secretly followed by his young son yet again. Eventually Hywel was successful. He'd surreptitiously crept up behind that tribal leader and was most surprised at the size of the person he'd been trailing.

On catching him up, red headed Berwyn fumed

with anger and raised his massive club. "Tired of living you horrid Ordovice are you? Over here to challenge me you've come, is it? Sent by that scheming brother, you've been too I suppose! Well, I'll soon show what to the likes of you I do!" He wielded his club but Hywel evaded his swipe.

On witnessing Berwyn's swing, Geraint, hiding in a hedge, held his breath. Although he had every faith in his father he was worried for his safety when confronted by that tremendously big man. The boy struggled with great difficulty to avoid giving a massive howl.

There then followed a lengthy battle with neither contestant getting a positive advantage. Berwyn was so amazed at his opponent's skill that he suddenly became surprised to find he had a limited respect for him. They continued to struggle until he determined to finish things quickly. He took one colossal swipe and, in hurriedly avoiding being hit, the Ordovice stumbled. As he did, he accidentally struck the enemy hard behind the knees. The heavy opponent hit the ground with such force he was totally winded and unable to rise for several minutes; unfortunately for him his powerful club had slipped from his grasp.

Hywel, quickly recovering from his stumble, stood threateningly over him.

Berwyn was amazed. He couldn't understand why he was being spared. Had the situation been reversed he'd have wasted no time in battering the man.

"Now perhaps reasonably we can speak," suggested Hywel. "Not to injure you I've come, but some friendly agreement to get for a change."

"No agreement ever with that barbarous brother of yours will I have!" He was showing quite as much stubbornness as Mawddach.

"To do with him, nothing this is. Not to my suggestion would he listen, so to you now I've come hoping more helpful you might be." He paused for a few minutes, thinking. "Like me, fed up with these horrible Romans penetrating your territory, you must be. Been interfering and upsetting us far too long now, haven't they?"

"Unable them to stop though, isn't it? Tried I have many times."

"On your own yes, but if a selected group from both tribes we form and properly trained we could possibly slow or halt their intrusions. Something worthwhile to try, that would be, don't you think?"

"With that hateful Mawddach you want me to unite, is it? Never!" he spat. "Trust him I don't – and never will! Some deceitful trick of his on me you're trying, and work it won't! Go back quick if you want to live, or my tribe will find you and deal with you! Tell that brother of yours that always trouble between us there'll be!"

Hywel realised he was having similar difficulty

with Berwyn as he'd had with Mawddach but he wasn't giving up. While he still had his victim on the ground, despite noting the look of intense hatred in his eyes, he was determined to continue. "Not being reasonable you are," he said. "Killed you I could have, but spared you I have, see. Not hate, that must show."

The Deceangli chief very reluctantly accepted the argument as he vainly struggled to rise but Hywel remained, threatening. "What to do, you intend then?" he queried pretentiously trying to conceal his impatience, for even at that stage he still hoped to overcome his opponent.

"A troublesome group from both tribes we could form. Pester and trouble the Romans wherever they are and hopefully reduce their aggressions. It would be a lot better than all this fighting between us, for we're still all Celtic people aren't we?"

The red headed leader was still most stubbornly opposed. "Not see that working, I can. Said before, that Mawddach I don't trust!"

"Happy to let the Romans do to your land what they like, you are then? Wasting my time I've been, it seems! Never rid of these foreigners we'll be, unless unite our tribes we do."

There was a noticeable reduction of hate in the big leader's eyes. Was he reluctantly thinking about it, or considering something else?

Hywel decided that was the best he could have

expected, so quickly departed before Berwyn had time to get up, or he was found by Deceangli tribesmen. As he went he was pondering how he could have better argued when he heard a desperate call.

"Tad! Tad!" On turning he was amazed to find his child desperately attempting to catch him up. Despite loving his youngster immensely and silently admiring the way he'd concealed himself, Hywel severely chastised him for his naughtiness and the risk he'd taken.

Surprisingly both had been completely unaware of another intruder. The sneaky rat-faced Tyddyn Fach, the snooping informer of Mawddach himself had also been involved. Tyddyn Fach never failed to report all unusual happenings to his chief for he was always hoping to receive favours.

Berwyn had also been pondering. He considered it could be a possible proposition which, if successful, would later give him the opportunity to tackle Mawddach even more fiercely and hopefully get rid of that terrible Ordovice neighbour forever.

Although Hywel had wasted no time in returning, Tyddyn Fach had made sure to arrive before him. The small informer had been determined to enlighten his leader regarding what had transpired at the earliest possible moment. "With that dangerous Berwyn Goch your brother has been," he stated hurriedly. He'd been determined to reveal Hywel's action at the earliest possible moment. "Trying to be friendly with him, he was. Told him with the Deceanglis to join, he wants us. Big trouble for us that will make, won't it?" He was certainly stirring it up. Fractionally over five feet tall and as thin as a spear shaft the insignificant interfering Ordovice trembled whenever he stood before his Chief.

"Sure, you are?" demanded a ranting Mawddach shaking him like the rat he was. The chief's massive dog, disturbed by the noise, growled as it attempted to rise. Its owner kicked savagely at it. "Down, lie!" he raved.

"Saw and heard them myself I did," affirmed the now terrified informer.

When Hywel came into sight accompanied by Geraint, his outraged elder sibling stormed at him. "Cythral!" he cursed with aggressively protruding eyes and saliva issuing from his quivering mouth. "No authority to approach that murderous Deceangli in the name of this tribe, you had! Pity he didn't kill you!" His facial fungus wobbled aggressively and the heavy wooden stick stabbed close to his brother's chest. Mawddach shook with anger. The wolfhound raised its upper lip in a snarl to support its master's tone, exposing its fangs once more. "Down lie!" its owner screamed again as he struck the dog with the stick. The subdued animal slowly obeyed with a look of hate in its eyes. "Challenged my authority you did then?" he ranted. "Lead the tribe, you think you can now, is it? For disloyalty like that, staked to the ground you should be!" There was every indication that he strongly regretted being unable to do it. "Not until a twig like this on that crow emblem you have will you control this tribe!" he yelled, "– and even that shouldn't save you now for what you've done!" His vindictiveness was most pronounced. It revealed quite clearly that he'd have been delighted to impose the ultimate penalty on him. He stabbed furiously at his brother's feet but Hywel didn't flinch and the rod landed a mere inch from his latticed leg.

The younger Cadwaladr was fully aware of the risk he'd taken for he'd often seen prominent members of the tribe pegged to the ground through Mawddach's terrific anger. They'd been left to an agonisingly slow death for the pettiest objection to their ruthless leader's demands.

Firmly grabbing Geraint before his brother had time to answer, Mawddach added, "Not spare you or this horrible child that crow will, even if my brother you are!" He poked at the boy who winced and as the father made a move to rescue him he was stopped, for the Ordovice Chief was holding a knife to the youngster's throat. That venomous threat indicated yet again that Mawddach would have been pleased to exterminate them both. "Total allegiance from everyone I demand – and from you too that is! No respect at all to me you show, and this revolting child, to be like yourself you've encouraged!"

Geraint struggled to release himself from his terrifying uncle, wishing he was old enough to strike him for upsetting his tad. The hound snarled threateningly again and the boy swiftly backed away to be returned to Mawddach's grabbing arms. The tribal leader seemed sufficiently satisfied not to check the animal as the fear in the youngster's eyes greatly pleased him.

"To that wicked Deceangli again straight away you'll go!" he screamed. "No agreement with him there is to be, tell him! Not with that savage leader under any circumstances we are joining. No terms with them will I ever accept. To act in the name of this tribe again without my authority you will not! Being my brother next time won't save you – so don't forget that!" He'd continued to hold the dagger to the young boy's throat. "Quick go you will now. Take Tyddyn Fach. See you do it properly he will, and tell me." The dog grumbled yet again as Hywel took a step to defend his son. The youngster's eyes pleaded desperately, but the father was forced back by his yell, uncertain whether the blade had been inserted. The hound growled aggressively again. "Down!" screamed its master stabbing the stick in the dog's direction once more. The subdued animal's eyes showed hate as it rapidly withdrew. "Not see this child again you will until Tyddyn tells me you've done things right."

"One day for this you black hearted scoundrel will pay!" yelled Hywel as he turned to go.

"Soon, not in a position that threat to make perhaps you'll be," sneered the elder brother. His mind was already working on the hope that if only he could inform the Romans of his sibling's movements and intentions, they could possibly remove him. "Might not be too long either, see," he added spitefully with a stentorian guffaw. His hopes had certainly started to climb.

CHAPTER
II

Darkness was falling and despite fearing for his son's safety Hywel knew his brother would accept no delay. Although not happy at having to relay the news to Berwyn, after such a hard struggle he was still uncertain whether he'd won his support. He knew he'd have to make a confession that he'd come with a complete reversal of his former suggestion. There was no knowing how the Deceangli chief would react to that, and Hywel feared he'd probably interpret it as some devious scheme of Mawddach by his requesting him to unite with him in the first place. The chief's brother was certain that the sneaky Tyddyn would report his every movement, and, watched by an apprehensive young son in the grip of a sadistic uncle, he despondently left the camp in a north easterly direction with that detestable little rat-like creature detailed by his chief mere yards behind. Despite his heavy heart Hywel knew he'd had no choice. Unless he totally followed his brother's directive his young son would undoubtedly suffer and he'd be unable to prevent it.

Iorwerth Morgwn, having noticed the man he respected being openly trailed by that horrible

Tyddyn, rightly assumed something very serious was happening. Following uneasily at a distance, his doubts were quickly confirmed. His friend's movements had always been so positive and he'd regularly been accompanied by Geraint apart from when he'd been involved in skirmishes. Realising something serious must have happened the nineteen-year-old increased his pace and quickly caught up with the child's father. "The matter's what, Hywel?" he enquired quietly.

"To Berwyn Goch he's to go. Tell him not united with them we're going to be," offered the cheeky, interfering Tyddyn gloating with satisfaction as he impudently revealed he'd even overheard Iorwerth's whisper.

Iorwerth grabbed the informer by the throat. "When asked you are, then speak you can! Otherwise quiet keep, you snooping little rat."

Tyddyn gasped and rubbed his throat as Iorwerth released him. Iorwerth, having been trusted with Hywel's subdued whispered intentions, argued quietly that time, ensuring Tyddyn didn't hear. He stated there'd be a better chance of rescuing Geraint if he tried, rather than the father.

Reluctantly, Hywel agreed.

Requesting Hywel to keep the slippery Tyddyn under close observation Iorwerth sloped off into the night. Rounding up some forty tribesmen who were willing to join Hywel, he selected two. Together they stealthily entered the chief's compound in the dead of night and silently disabling the child's guard they scooped up the lad and returned him to his father.

When all the accompanying tribesmen were informed of what had happened, they supported Hywel's suggested arrangement with Berwyn Goch and instantly threw in their lot with him.

Learning of that, Tyddyn escaped.

Making their way towards Deceangli territory the group were suddenly surrounded by almost a hundred marauding Deceanglis. Believing they were approaching their tribal land as a prelude to an attack, they scoffed at Hywel's explanation that he wanted to see Berwyn.

"We're certain that our chief will be delighted to see you!" laughed the leading man sarcastically. "Quite sure of that, we are!" he added with an enormous grin.

The Ordovices were rounded up and escorted to the Deceangli encampment.

Meanwhile the wily Tyddyn Fach had reached Mawddach with news of Geraint's release. The chief was enraged. He promptly sentenced the tribesman who'd guarded the boy to the ultimate penalty. His fury increased even more on learning that several of the tribe had deserted to Hywel. He swore that each one of them, along with his brother, would suffer when he caught up with them.

Two days later the escorted group reached Berwyn's compound. They'd traversed small rivers, skirted several lakes and eventually crossed the Conwy itself. After wading through, they'd turned in a northerly direction to access Deceangli country and reached a prominent hill fort near Nebo. The extensive unrestricted panoramic views to the west completely amazed Hywel. Passing through a well-guarded entrance they were confronted by Berwyn Goch himself. Hearing Hywel's message he flew into a rage, accusing him of treachery and deceit. "About joining together, lies you told me!" he howled. "Not Romans fighting it was to be, but preparing for another Ordovice attack you were! To spy this time as well you've come! Bad as that wicked brother you are! Now at my mercy, you'll see what to enemies we really do! Ordovice trick this is!" scowled Berwyn. "Seize them!"

Geraint, held in the firm grip of an opposition tribesman, watched with alarm. His little legs trembled with fear as he saw his father offer no resistance.

"The truth I tell you," insisted Hywel passionately without raising his voice. "Spared you when at my mercy I had you, didn't I? For that alone, believe me you must. If more Deceanglis amongst the Rebels than Ordovices there are, then treachery cannot happen."

"Save you that won't. Take more of my tribesmen away to weaken us now you want," Berwyn accused.

"My cherished son as hostage I'll leave to prove

I'm serious." Hywel studied Berwyn carefully and on seeing his doubt appearing to waver, looked lovingly at his child to comfort and reassure him.

Although Geraint completely trusted his father his little heart beat fiercely. He squirmed as he waited to see if Hywel's offer would be accepted. The last thing he wanted to be was a hostage. He ached to dash into his father's arms but knew that the stakes were far too high.

The furious looking Red Berwyn considered things for some time and Hywel was uncertain whether he'd accept. He was tempted to withdraw, but the safety of his child and the accompanying group was at risk and he wasn't prepared to sacrifice them. When the pugnacious Deceangli leader first received news that Mawddach had rejected the merger he was furious as it had upset his hoped-for eventual outcome. "To fight now, not good enough he thinks I am! Better than him ten times we are," he declared proudly. "The whole fighting tribe ready get now!" he screeched to his follower. He was about to launch an immediate attack on his enemy and Hywel had to use all his persuasive power to prevent him storming off.

"Not worry about him, you should," Hywel pleaded, insisting such action would only help the Romans. Geraint's father argued so fiercely that eventually he persuaded the Deceangli leader against the undertaking. Berwyn's final agreement to form a specialised unit, as Hywel had suggested, had taken a considerable amount of time and the Mynydd Rebels were to be formed, with Hywel as leader. There was a stern directive to be successful for the sake of the child. The Deceangli tribesmen who joined were firmly instructed to keep sharp watchful eyes on him.

Once established, the Mynydd Rebels unmercifully pestered the Romans who'd so contemptuously infiltrated into their beloved Cymru. They'd often sweep down from Moel Siabod or Glydir Fawr before retreating into the wild hinterlands. At times, they'd travel further east into Deceangli territory to disturb the Romans more. On other occasions, they'd withdraw into the covering recesses of Mynydd Hiraethog. Their achievements had hindered the invaders to an annoying degree and Hywel had eventually been identified as the leader. A couple of times he'd been caught and it had maddened the Roman centurion Flavius that he'd managed to escape. A special reward was being offered to the Roman who finally exterminated Hywel, and Flavius was determined to achieve that.

Hywel had planned things to perfection. He'd witnessed a Roman cohort making for Sir Fon. They'd be collecting gold and, roughly knowing when they'd be returning, he'd carefully prepared an intrusion, patiently biding his time. True to his usual practice he'd informed only a select few of the details, but he was unaware that the devious Tyddyn had snooped again.

On that day Hywel had been hiding behind a large boulder on Tryfan studying the movement of the Roman cohort making its way to Segontium. Segontium overlooked his beloved Mona ('Mam Cymru') and he'd always considered that island the mother of Wales. The Romans seemed determined to keep to the route regardless of any possible intervention. It was extremely important for them as they regularly transported large quantities of Welsh gold extracted from Caer y Cwr, a small island situated east of Mona. The returning cohort had been some distance away when Hywel had first spotted it and he'd awaited his chance.

That was the type of situation Mawddach had waited for and as soon as he was aware of it he concentrated on arranging a treacherous betrayal of his brother. By devious means he'd informed the Romans and they'd arranged the trap.

Waiting carefully as usual, Hywel finally spotted the returning cohort still some distance off. Then he noticed an elderly looking man emerge from a large copse quite a way down. He was carrying a sizeable bundle of wood and when he slipped he seemed unable to get up. As the Romans were soon approaching and fearing he'd be in extreme danger, Hywel hurried down the mountain to assist him. As he bent over him, the man grabbed him and several concealed soldiers emerged from the copse. They held him firm and thrust him to the ground.

That had been the moment when Flavius was approaching, and on realising it was Hywel he drew his sword and kicked his horse into a canter. One member of the legion was in the way. One time previously that Roman had been spared by Hywel when he'd been seriously wounded, and in the black of night the Celt had courageously struggled with him to the nearest fort leaving him within a reasonable distance of its entrance in the hope that he'd be found. His charitable act had been successful and that legionnaire, who'd also recognised Hywel, intended to repay his generosity by stepping in Flavius' way to prevent such a savage act. The centurion was so determined to eliminate Hywel that he kicked at the legionnaire. "Out of my way, you scum!" he yelled before he plunged his sword into the prostrate body time after time.

Hywel's followers stared in disbelief. All of them were awestruck when they realised their leader was unlikely to rise again. Iorwerth Morgwn, Hywel's most devoted follower, cursed. He sadly regretted not having been near enough to attempt a rescue, though under the circumstances he'd not have been able to save him. Even a full muster of Rebels would have failed. They'd been too far up the mountainside even to have attempted it.

Mawddach, watching from higher up, grinned. He was completely satisfied.

CHAPTER
III

As Geraint lay in despair, it suddenly dawned on him that he now had no family to speak of. That upset him much more and his crying increased. The realisation that his sole remaining relative was his brutal uncle Mawddach, who'd never shown any affection for him, disturbed him immensely. The tribal chief had never concealed his detestation for the young boy. Realising that, the lad was suddenly filled with fear: his future seemed positively grim.

Mawddach had been unaware of his nephew's presence until the tragedy had been performed. Then when Geraint had made such a screaming noise, his chief's attention had been suddenly directed to him. The uncle had been some distance above Geraint with his wolfhound beside him as usual, but he'd quickly skirted down and wickedly grabbed hold of the boy. "Stop all that horrible noise!" he yelled, striking him with his stick.

The child's howls became intense. "Leave me alone!" he shrieked. "Don't you know Tad's just been killed?"

"That's what he's deserved for a long time!"

Mawddach spitefully showed no sympathy and hit the youngster again. The howling became more extreme.

The dreadful attack by the Roman had also been witnessed from a distance by Iorwerth who had been alongside the Rebels, and upon hearing Geraint's penetrating wails looked up to see Mawddach striking young Geraint who'd just lost a dear father. He immediately became incensed and made all haste to accost his chief. "Whatever are you doing to that boy, you villain?" he called as he was approaching. "Can't you appreciate the tremendous agony he must be in after just seeing his father so brutally slain? Have you no respect or decency at all? You're a proper beast!"

"No talking to me like that I'll have! Respect from you it will be, or suffer you will!" There wasn't the slightest sign of sympathy for the youngster and that maddened Iorwerth more.

"Iorwerth, save me!" screamed the child as the dog lurched to attack him but Mawddach yanked him back and the animal's exertion ended in choking coughs as it was arrested in mid-air by a powerful pull on its leash.

"Deal with him myself, I will – not you!" he howled at the beast. "Up brat, get!" yelled the Ordovice leader to the bereaved youngster on the ground. He yanked the dog's lead once more as the animal again jerked forward. "Down!" he cried with uncontrolled temper.

The animal gasped again. "Not to be savaged he is until I tell you!" The hound raised its upper lip and bared its teeth at its master. It was rewarded with another vicious kick which caused it to yelp again. "Show your teeth to me, then dare you?" he screamed at the dog.

Iorwerth approached, and there was a massive verbal confrontation which led to his banishment from the tribe. Iorwerth knew he would have incurred the ultimate penalty had he struck his leader and, even though he'd been very tempted, he couldn't risk such a drastic penalty as he'd have been no use to the boy then.

"Out of my sight get before the punishment you deserve I inflict upon you!" He'd love to have imposed that on him but with the Mynydd Rebels rapidly approaching and Mawddach being alone he was fearful of them. He grabbed the boy by his jerkin and yanked him to his feet. "With me you're coming now and behave yourself you'll have to."

"Help me Iorwerth," pleaded the boy more painfully that time.

Iorwerth was so enraged that he wanted to, but his chief's threat had stopped him. Instead he shamefully watched the youngster being hauled further up the Welsh mountain and away from him by his vicious uncle. Although little Geraint's legs were weak and he could hardly stand it made no difference. Mawddach encouraged the dog to move faster as he wickedly dragged at the boy more fiercely.

"Hurting me, my legs are," he complained.

"Hurt you more they will if you don't move quicker," he snarled.

"Diawl. Hate you I do!" wailed the youngster aggressively in a mournful high pitched tone. There was no hiding the feeling of disrespect bordering on open insolence. "Alone leave me, can't you? Bully you are and hate you I do!" he shrieked between sobs. "Not dare hit me like this if Tad was here you would!" the young Ordovice cried.

Still holding tightly onto the hound, Mawddach tugged at the youngster. "Not here your father is, and proper respect to me you'll give now! Not insolence like this I'll take from you! 'Chief' too, you'll call me always!" His yelling thunderous voice re-echoed loudly around those majestic mountains.

"Not, I will!" The child was firmly defiant. His uncle shook him savagely. "Hated me and Tad always you have; yet belong to you we do!" Geraint screamed, despite his intense pain. "Get off me! Leave me alone! Big bully you are! Hate you I do! Iorwerth I want!" The youngster was revealing his most offensive defiance with an unmistakable tremor in his voice. He unsuccessfully tried to strike his uncle and in so doing tripped over a rock and severely damaged his knee. The hound bared its teeth and issued an unpleasant growl. Geraint forced his head down to conceal his weakness from his uncle as tears cascaded from his eyes. "Hurt, I am," he cried. "Let me go!"

"More hurt you'll be, if up you don't get!"

"Not if Tad was here, you'd say that!"

"Not here he is now – and never will be again," crowed Mawddach again inflicting as much sorrow on the boy as he could.

Geraint's agony was most pronounced; there was a decided quiver in his voice. Forcing himself up, with tears streaming down his face, he again unsuccessfully tried to attack his chief. The hound lurched forward again and was pulled sharply back a mere fraction from the boy who received another stinging blow for his insolence. It knocked him over once more.

"Interfering always your father was and no trouble from you I'll take! In full charge I am and total respect from you I'll have as well! Nobody to watch and interfere now there is, so how I treat you I decide!" His sneer was disgusting and the child's little body heaved as the unchecked tears flowed far more freely. The hound bounded to the end of its shortened tether but was unable to reach him. Geraint bit his bottom lip in a brave endeavour to avoid crying, and it drew blood.

"Deserved all he got for disobeying me Hywel did, and to follow in his unruly ways like this you want too, is it? Severe punishment you'll get if you do! Call me 'Chief' always you will now!" he stated again. "Up, get!" he commanded as he attempted to kick him. The weakened lad had half expected the kick and just managed to roll out of reach in time, flattening the nearby ferns as he went. Bitterly pining the loss of his father and aching for the friendship of Iorwerth, he knew he'd never forget that situation and longed for the day when he'd be big enough to really tackle his cruel uncle.

The youngster was continuously pummelled and prodded as he was forced up Tryfan. He was staggering and struggling on weakened legs all the way and there was no possible means of escape. He felt totally inadequate to the situation imposed upon him and he simply wanted to flop onto the friendly looking earth and never rise again, but he certainly wasn't allowed to for Mawddach's punishing cruelty didn't ease.

"Let me stop!" screamed Geraint in an excessive high pitch but his plea of desperation was ignored by his sadistic uncle who, with increased brutality, pulled at him to make him move even faster. The numerous scattered tussocks concealing the rocky surfaces greatly hindered the boy's progress. With aching knees and deadened legs, he found it very difficult to cope. Exhaustion rapidly overtook him and he repeatedly tripped. The further they went the more strenuous and difficult the going became. Mawddach's annoyance increased. Due to his nephew's frequent falls their progress had been drastically slowed.

Approaching Glydir Fawr on the right they were within sight of the Celtic priest's hutment. It was partly concealed by a few isolated trees but Peris the Druid, having spotted them, came out to admonish the heartless Ordovice leader. Wrapping his green vestment tightly about himself he stepped into the chilling wind. Geraint's hopes rose as he saw the religious man approaching.

"Help me, please!" he begged with a voice conveying anguish. "Hurting me all the time he's been!" It resulted in another severe cuff across the ear from his uncle. "Ow!" yelled the child as the vicious blow hit.

"That boy leave alone Mawddach Du! Let him come to me!" ordered Peris.

"By what authority do you order that?" demanded the Ordovice chief. "My charge he is – not yours!"

"Release him in the name of decency," persisted the priest.

"Not your business this is Druid, and with respect you'll address me properly too! To your religion only look – and not to what I do!

The sage was not subdued. "For the boy, my concern is. Ashamed a person in your position should be for treating him like that! Far too young to suffer so unnecessarily he is, especially after what he's just been through! His welfare is more important than your bloated pomposity. Pay for this one day Mawddach Du you will!"

"Pay yourself will too, if not careful you are! My responsibility this boy now is and no interference from you, I'll take!" The violent tempered uncle hurriedly thrust the boy forward before the priest could chastise him further. Peris shook his head in disbelief as they moved away.

Nearing Glydir Fach to the left as darkness was descending they stopped beside a craggy outcrop on the exposed mountainside. There was a solitary mountain ash to accompany them for the night. Mawddach firmly secured the youngster's hands and feet with strong fronds to prevent any attempt to escape. Having had nothing to eat, Geraint's little stomach was craving for food but Mawddach didn't seem to care.

"Hungry I am," complained the boy.

"Your fault for not moving faster that is!" he responded at his most venomous. "Home now we'd be if not so slow you'd been!"

Geraint spent a miserable night on the open mountainside. Pangs of hunger had regularly gnawed at his stomach. A few feet away the tethered dog issued a threatening deep throated rumble every time the boy shifted his aching limbs. Rain fell in the early hours and he writhed with increased discomfort.

Nothing seemed to reduce the aches and pains in his hands and feet, and every time he made a complaint he was further abused. Desperation forced him to avoid additional protests as he became determined not to give Mawddach any extra satisfaction. Instead he gallantly clenched his teeth, forcing himself to endure the agony in silence.

Freed from his bonds next morning, he rubbed his aching limbs to restore the circulation but even then, he wasn't allowed time. His callous uncle forced him to move before he was fully eased. Every time he stumbled or fell on his rigid legs he was immediately kicked and hauled up.

"Help it, I can't!" he cried. "Tied my hands and feet too tight you did! Still numb they are now!

"Move quicker then, and normal again soon they'll be." Mawddach Du's inhumanity didn't reduce. Every time his nephew complained it brought on more punishment.

Geraint continued to slip and stagger on the numerous patches of loose scree scattered intermittently down a very steep slope. Within minutes they were looking down a very narrow pass. He registered the large rocks that rose on either side. Too frequently the boy was unable to safely negotiate the treacherous slippery lichen-covered surfaces. His legs, limp from the extremely gruelling journey, repeatedly gave way beneath him the further they descended. Every time he fell, grazing his already damaged knee even more, he cried out in agony causing his impatient uncle's temper to increase.

"Up, get! Stand on your feet!" he yelled pitilessly. "Not like us to me you are when childish you act!" The dog's upper lip curled as if in support of its master's rebuke.

They reached the Nant with difficulty then faced a long arduous climb on the steep side of Wyddfa. They were heading for Mawddach's secluded encampment near Llyn Llydaw where the Ordovice leader would have a completely uninterrupted view of any impending attacks from the north east. On the way, they'd passed an odd little lake and several small copses. The rest was made up of extremely dangerous lichen covered rock. Small pockets of scree with the occasional patch of fern also appeared. From the manner in which he'd arranged his compound it was apparent that Mawddach had always been fearful of the Deceanglis, yet he seemed determined to be permanently at war with them despite his brother's attempt to unify the tribes.

CHAPTER
IV

The two days' strenuous journey had been complete purgatory. Geraint had delayed his uncle's progress which had caused his fury to mount beyond belief. Not only had the boy been wet, cold and miserable, he'd also been starved. He'd eaten only a few wild berries and been continually mistreated. Mists had started to envelop them for much of the remaining part of the way: the clouds had created a frightening eeriness beneath a dismally overcast late summer sky. The barren area had been completely foreign to him. It had been most uninviting and made him feel scared. He was completely alone and uncared for. They finally arrived at Mawddach's well defended enclosure. He'd had very little respite throughout the journey: he was hungry and weary and bordering on collapse, convinced he couldn't go any further.

"To light a fire, some wood now you must get before eat or rest you do," dictated the sadistic uncle who seemed satisfied to see the exhausted state of the youngster.

"Hungry and tired I am," he wailed dolefully. "First to eat something I want!"

"Eat, you tell me!" the bullying chief screamed. "Tell the great Mawddach Du what to do dare you? On your knees too when something you want, you'll go! Respect show me now when speak you will!"

He pushed the boy to the ground again. The dog growled and the lad's spirit gave way.

"Very hungry I am," he cried pathetically, fighting unsuccessfully to stem his tears.

"Call me 'Chief', you will" snarled Mawddach.

"Ch-ief," the feeble childish voice sullenly revealed his reluctance.

"Louder!" screamed Mawddach.

"Chief," repeated Geraint slightly more strongly, "and still hungry I am!" His bottom lip quivered as he struggled feebly to make his point.

"Hungry too until that wood you get, you'll be!" He meant to subdue him as quickly as possible. He knocked him to the floor again.

"From where do I get it?" he enquired, trying to rise on wobbly legs. He still harboured a tendency to disrespect.

"Chief!" screamed his raging uncle pushing him to his knees again.

"Ch-ief," repeated the lad slightly more firmly, his voice croaking with fear.

"Find out things for yourself, you'll have to from now on." The reply was unhelpful. "Nothing to eat you'll have until enough wood you've got!" He was determined to break the boy.

Geraint lowered his head as he tried to secretly wipe away his flowing tears. He bravely tried not to show weakness to his vile relative. He moved away as fast as his aching legs would carry him; tears cascaded yet again. Feeling totally miserable, weary, and unwanted he was forced to pause every few yards. With nobody to see him he let his tears flow freely; his groaning was excessive. Although somewhat sturdy, his little body vibrated with agony. Events were far too much for him, yet he couldn't avoid them. His tears shamed him. It upset him to realize that his dear father would have been disappointed to see him in such a weakened state.

Slowly arriving at a clearing within the darkened copse he sat despondently on a felled log. He believed that his little world was completely disintegrating and howled uncontrollably. Life had suddenly become immensely cruel and with nobody to see his misery he'd completely passed the point of caring. He seemed to lose all hope and his interest in living was quickly disappearing.

Although there was an abundance of loose wood, he realised it would be too bulky and heavy to carry up that steep incline. He was hungry and weary and far too weak to carry even the smaller pieces. Total despair overcame him and his sobbing increased.

Miserably he reflected on the unfairness of his young life as he wondered how he'd be able to collect sufficient wood to prevent further punishment. He sat and wailed miserably, feebly kicking at the moss adhering to a nearby log. Frustration overcame him. Suddenly a grubby-faced, fair-headed girl about two years his elder seemed to appear from nowhere.

"What the matter is, bachgen?" Her question showed genuine concern. With such a tender and friendly tone, the girl brought an unexpected sense of relief. With her appearance, he desperately struggled to restrict his tears. "Miserable, proper you look now, bach. Upset you what has then?" It was the first sign of concern he had received since Iorwerth – and that lamentable tragedy that had caused such an abundance of misery. After that, everything seemed to get worse and worse.

Despite an attempt to control himself, tears of thankfulness rolled down his face. She'd brought such unexpected friendliness it made him feel ashamed. Being desperately in need of a friend he certainly wanted her to be one. He hoped that what seemed like childish weakness wouldn't put her off. With a warm tender arm curled around his heaving hunched shoulders she attempted to comfort him. He rubbed his eyes in a further attempt to stem his tears. Not wanting this kindly girl to see him as a baby, he forced himself to look up at her. With tearful courage and a wan smile, he considered her grime-smeared face which appeared to display a strong, maternal, sympathy.

Realising the child was at the end of his tether she became eager to console him. "Come on," she encouraged gently. "Not that bad it is. Big lad you are now see! Brave you must be!"

"B-but, tir-ed and hung-ry, I am," he confessed in sorrowful gasps as he failed to stop snivelling. "Lo-ts of w-ood to get I've got to! Car-ry it all up there, I ca-n't". He pointed in the general direction.

"Worry not, bach. Help you I will." She paused. "Look, Alwena, I am. What name is yours?"

"Ger-aint," he offered as his sobbing started again. "Mur-der-ed by the Romans my ta-d has just been." He sucked his breath despondently, "And no-body to look after me now I've got!"

"Nice name is Geraint. Look after you, if stop crying you do, I will." She was immediately sympathetic towards the dishevelled black-haired boy. His pitiful eyes were completely drained of fun. The innocence of his face increased her compassion. "How old you are, then?" she enquired, determined to help this desperately sad youngster.

"Ei-ght," he sniffed again.

"Ten, I am," she announced proudly in a tone suggesting she was far more mature than her age. "Tell me about you, then friends we will be, isn't it?" Her sympathy was extended further when between his sobs, he detailed his misfortunes. Her eyes welled too as she was reminded of her own problems. She knew just how cruel the Romans could be, for her spirited father had been captured and severely tortured by a similar group of invaders and left to die. Fortunately though, he'd survived, and as a helpless cripple he was no further threat to them. As a result of his injuries, he'd become totally dependent on his young daughter for everything. Everyone knew of Black Mawddach's callous reputation: his heartless intolerance was a legend throughout the whole region.

"Bad one our chief is," she said.

Geraint cried, "Know that I do! Never enough wood to please him I'll get. Too tired to carry it up to Llyn Llydaw I am, anyway."

Disregarding her own sadness, at the sight of his misery she endeavoured to encourage him. "Come on. Help you to carry enough, I will. All up the mountain too I'll carry it for you if stop crying you do!" She showed him where to find the best wood and taught him how to bind it in large bundles with creepers pulled from the trees.

He found comfort in the company of the young girl who was only slighter taller than himself. Her presence temporarily relieved his despondency and he quickly developed a wish that she would stay with him always. He watched her with amazement as she rapidly strapped up two large bundles and effortlessly slung them across her narrow back. Although he had nothing to carry, he found the return journey uphill difficult enough as his aching legs were hardly supporting him. He realised he'd never have made it without her assistance and her presence had suddenly given him a sense of encouragement.

As they neared Mawddach's hut the bullying uncle stormed out at them. "You to collect the wood I told! Not a cheeky looking girl like this!" He picked up a stick and turned on Alwena. "Away!" he yelled, raising the stick threateningly. The tethered hound also registered its disapproval. "Not around here to see you again I want or this stick you'll get!" The terrified girl started to flee as he made to hit her. "Not around here you're to be!" he repeated as she went. He yelled at Geraint. "On your knees go – and sorry you'll say too!" He turned on the girl again. Concerned for the boy, she'd stopped some distance away looking petrified. "Flogged I'll have you if go you don't!" Alwena needed no further warning. Feeling sorry for the terrible situation of that lovely looking child she hurried away, frightened that her despicable leader wouldn't hesitate in applying his threat. That had made her move. Regardless, she was determined to see Geraint again but didn't know how.

Charging at Geraint, Mawddach thrust him to the ground again. "To your knees, you'll go, I said!" The boy lay prostrate. Unable to contain himself any longer he sobbed bitterly. Things had been drastic enough: losing his father was extremely bad and then Iorwerth. Now this newly found girl he'd hoped would become his friend had also been sent away. It seemed there was absolutely nobody for him to turn to.

"That snivelling childish noise at once stop!" ordered his uncle. Roughly dragging him into the corner of the hut, he thrashed him unmercifully with a stick. The traumatised child was past protest. He could neither yell nor move. Defenceless, he cowered in agony on the floor, awaiting the comfort of oblivion. The dog grumbled threateningly nearby, as his bruised little body heaved with sobs. It worried him. With a savage determination he hoped for the day when he'd be big enough to repay his callous uncle – and he vowed that it would be with interest.

CHAPTER
V

Initially Mawddach, resolved to break his nephew's stubbornness, was determined not to feed him. Later he decided to punish him even more with a bowl of rancid stew. It contained bits of putrid meat which should have been thrown out. Although desperately hungry, Geraint found the smell too obnoxious and stood staring sullenly at it. His uncle exploded. "Hungry, you said you was – all of it eat up then, you will!"

"Bu-t sme-lls horr-ible it does!" the lad protested.

"Eat it!" commanded Mawddach angrily. His instruction was so intense that Geraint was forced to try eating it and his uncle's annoyance eased slightly.

"Ugh! Not fit for a dog it is," grumbled the boy peevishly as he continued to dawdle over it.

"Eat it!" bellowed his uncle banging his hand on the table so hard that the bowl bounced. "Not to waste food you are, and when talking to me you say 'Chief'!" he screamed. "Chief!" shouted Mawddach again. "Horrible? Horrible that food is you say? Until it's all eaten up nothing more you'll get!" He strode out in temper.

The dog lying in the corner grieved for attention

but not surprisingly its master ignored it.

With his uncle out of sight Geraint quickly spat the unpleasant food out of his mouth. He hadn't particularly directed it anywhere but by chance it landed near to the severely underfed animal. The hound slowly eased itself onto its legs and ambled across to investigate. After an initial sniff at the morsel it turned up its nose as if to confirm Geraint's statement that it wasn't fit for a dog. It paused uncertainly and looked beseechingly at the lad for several minutes, then realising nothing better was forthcoming he slowly licked it up.

Having seen it disappear, Geraint hurriedly tossed the remaining few pieces, which the permanently undernourished hound eventually took with gratitude. Desperate for company of any sort Geraint tentatively moved nearer the wolfhound. Nervously he offered his hand and following a low growl of uncertainty the animal strolled over. It slowly placed its drooping chin pleadingly on the boy's knee and Geraint was amazed. It was the first indication of anything resembling affection since Alwena, and the animal's former aggression towards him seemed to have disappeared.

The meat had been sparse but the dog had accepted what little there was. Although desperately hungry, Geraint had to be satisfied with the remaining flavourless watery liquid, accompanied by a piece of dirty looking hard crust which did nothing to relieve his hunger. Despite not being pleasant, at least it was better than nothing and was a questionable improvement on that foul-tasting meat he'd given to the dog.

When Mawddach returned, the dog strolled dejectedly back to its corner in an attitude of submission and issued a subdued growl. "Down!" screamed Mawddach severely and the dog buried its head in its paws as it curled its lip threateningly in the corner, spying its master through one eye.

Geraint's uncle was quite surprised to see the empty bowl. "There," he scoffed, "eat what I give you always you will or starve!"

Things didn't improve for the nephew as he continued to endure unlimited abuse, but at least he had the comfort of the hound whenever Mawddach wasn't around. The animal would let him stroke and fondle it and, vicious though it could be, it was strangely terrified of its cruel master. Often it found comfort in the youngster's friendship and seemed to sense their association had to be hidden from Mawddach.

Geraint certainly had Alwena's support. Despite Mawddach's aggressive threat she still managed to meet him. Although inconsolable when she'd been forbidden to see him, her determination finally became effective. By watching carefully for several days, hiding behind strategically placed boulders, she discovered a way to continue their association. Knowing Mawddach was away she threw a stone and the boy became ecstatic when he saw her waving. At their first meeting, they devised a series of locations for clandestine follow-ups and their friendship became firmly established.

Alwena was a very patient listener. He had someone he could unburden his grief on for she was always extremely supportive. He related all the injustices and punishments he'd received from his uncle and disclosed how much he hated him. Despite his unhappiness, he was determined not to run away for a very special reason – he wanted to wait until he could punish him severely for all his dastardly deeds.

Whenever Geraint set out to meet Alwena the wolfhound, strangely, seemed to sense the mission and strained at its leash to join them. Geraint would have enjoyed its company but feared the Ordovice leader's undoubted reprisal on the dog which had now become a friend. Regrettably he was forced to ignore the canine's plea. It would have delighted him to be able to boast of both secret affairs but he was scared that Mawddach's anger would be levelled at both the dog and Alwena.

Over the years, he and the girl had spent hours together with Alwena encouraging him to develop his physique in several ways. They'd cavorted through the extensive copse where they'd first met, dodging between trees or hiding from each other. It had cultivated both his stamina and his powers of detection.

On one occasion, as a nine-year-old, he'd been standing on a rock above Llyn Llydaw's cold water when her unexpected push plunged him into the lake. The shock of the extremely icy water wrenched the breath from his body and in panic he desperately thrashed out. "O-h! O-h! Dr-own-ing I am!" he called in desperate short gasps, his chin juddering uncontrollably as he started to sink.

Alwena hadn't considered the possibility of his being unable to swim. She'd been terrified to see him go under. Forcing herself into the freezing water which also took her breath away she grabbed him and together they struggled to the bank. "Learn to swim now you must!" she unsympathetically admonished the gasping youngster. "Out of trouble someday it might get you!" Geraint petrified by such an unpleasant experience was tempted to object but feared it would influence their association. They selected a spot well out of Mawddach's sight and in all weathers he entered the lake daily. Once over the initial shock, he regularly enjoyed the experience. Gradually his chest and lungs became more powerful.

She taught him the art of spearing a fish with a pointed stick, then killing it with a sharp blow to the head. She then showed him how to make a fire and cook it so that he wouldn't go hungry. Knowing how desperately he wanted to avenge his father's memory Alwena was determined to toughen him up. The more powerful girl wrestled and grappled strongly with him and it gradually built up his muscles as he tried to better her. With her help, through many painful experiences, his physique became noticeably stronger. Acting as his life-line she became his only relief in an otherwise uneventfully miserable existence. Their association resulted in a strong brother-sister relationship which had developed quite naturally between them.

Not suspecting their connection, Mawddach had noticed his nephew's development but he wasn't worried. He was convinced that the hound would be able to track and recapture the youngster should he be foolish enough to attempt to escape. He didn't know the lad had no intention of fleeing until he could settle that terrible account with his uncle.

Alwena had given him every possible encouragement to strengthen himself and in his effort to please her he'd lifted increasingly heavy boulders. He'd started with smaller stones and gradually increased the size and weight until he'd really surprised himself. He'd also run extensive sections of the lakeside at increasing speeds, climbed the upper reaches of Wyddfa without his uncle's knowledge and his speed and stamina had vastly improved. Gradually, as his body developed, Mawddach's beatings seemed to become slightly more bearable. The lad was satisfied that his toughened body deprived his uncle of his former sadistic enjoyment. By feigned ready submission he'd let Mawddach believe he'd been tamed but he was still patiently awaiting his opportunity.

Slowly Mawddach became even more inhumane. He made several attempts to break the boy's spirit but his nephew became much bolder as he grew, and his confidence developed. His reactions became swifter; he stood his ground more boldly; never failed to show a deceitful pseudo element of respect. On the many occasions he challenged his uncle, he swiftly moved out of the way to avoid receiving the anticipated blow. Although still constantly bullied and threatened by Mawddach, Geraint was developing rapidly. As time went by, he became more able to accept the punishments. He showed the patience and endurance he'd inherited. He bore it all with stoicism as he eagerly looked forward to the day he could avenge his departed parent. There had been several opportunities for him to run away but he hadn't accepted them for they wouldn't have satisfied him. Besides he loathed the idea of leaving Alwena.

Throughout the years, he'd been determined to stick it out until he would be able to fully exact punishment for the treacherous way their leader had sacrificed his father. He'd been increasingly convinced that his uncle had been involved in his parent's wicked murder, and that thought being permanently on his mind had greatly increased his hatred. Mawddach had also been responsible for the unnecessary deaths of members of the tribe his father had befriended and his conviction that his uncle had informed the Romans, strengthened his resolve daily.

A time came for him to comfort Alwena. When her father eventually died, she became extremely depressed. "Without him, what to do I don't know," she sobbed. "Nobody else I've got now, see!"

"Me you've got, isn't it? Look after you, I will," he promised. "Looked after me long enough, you have."

About that time, the growing youngster came to realise that after Tyddyn's visits Mawddach would disappear in the depth of night. Following each of these periodic absences the leader would return in a more reasonable mood for a day or two before he resorted to his former contemptible self again. Such occasions were always forerunners of information relating to sizeable Deceangli defeats, the knowledge of which seemed to delight the big Ordovice leader. Surprisingly there was little rejoicing among many of his tribe, for their hatred of the Romans was much stronger than that of their fellow Celts. Fortunately, there'd been practically no trouble from Berwyn's tribe for some time as they'd been concentrating on attempting to hinder the Romans.

In the main, the Ordovicians had, with certain reservations, come to admire the improved skills of their rivals. However, the attempted copying of those skills which were associated with the Romans had resulted in only limited success against the invaders. There was a sense of jealousy among the tribe that the fellow Celts' achievements were somehow attributable to Hywel. They believed their former tribesman had taught the Deceanglis so many improvements they didn't possess by means of his association with the Rebels. That being the case, they were unable to understand why the infiltrators could still inflict such severe havoc on the Deceanglis. They appreciated that Hywel had been renowned for careful planning and were not surprised that his followers had to some degree mastered his techniques, yet they quietly suspected there'd been some sort of treachery.

Geraint's suspicions had taken the same course. They'd started to increase to such an extent that he had to confirm them. Sneaking out when all was quiet, using the cunning developed over the years with Alwena's help, he trailed Mawddach at a distance. Unsurprisingly the Ordovice leader made for the nearest Roman Hill Fort and the boy was truly amazed to see him enter, apparently unchallenged. It was as if he'd been expected by the hated Romans. The youngster was then in no doubt that it appeared to be something of a regular occurrence.

Days later he learned of another massive successful attack against the Deceanglis and for no accountable reason it had brought the horrible Flavius to mind once more. He believed it was due to his uncle somehow liaising with that dreadful centurion, that he'd come to detest so permanently, that his father had been murdered.

The Ordovician chief had never lost his hatred for Red Berwyn even though the Deceangli leader had concentrated mainly on the Romans. The neighbouring warring tribe's infiltrations into Ordovice territories had been considerably reduced. Geraint's uncle, it seemed, had conveyed information obtained by the sneaky Tyddyn Fach to the Romans. Consequently, the Deceangli fighting power was decreasing much to Mawddach's satisfaction. By his treachery, he'd gained a slight advantage from the invaders but was disappointed that Berwyn Goch had not been among the reported fatalities.

He forbade all members of the tribe to associate with kinsfolk who'd become Mynydd Rebels and offered a substantial reward for the capture of Iorwerth Morgwn.

From the age of ten the developing Geraint had reluctantly been forced to accompany the tribe in their assaults on the Deceanglis. Glued to his leader's side, he knew it wouldn't have been the wish of his father, for Hywel had struggled so desperately to unite the two tribes against the Romans and had paid the ultimate price. His father had eventually been accepted and trusted as a friend by the murderous Red Berwyn, which had been a tremendous achievement, and Geraint considered it disloyal to fight the Deceanglis now. The consciousness that Iorwerth might recognise him and believe he was condoning Mawddach's treachery, disturbed him. There was also the frightening possibility that Iorwerth could be killed by members of his own tribe and he certainly didn't want to witness that. He'd often thought he'd like to meet his father's former lieutenant but wondered if he'd recognise the sixteen-year-old boy he'd last seen some eight years previously.

With the passing of time he'd become much more daring in his meetings with Alwena. As powerfully built teenagers, they'd been discussing his uncle's attitude to them both, vowing they wouldn't let it happen again. Suddenly, to their surprise, Mawddach came across their hiding place. "Found both of you now, I have!" he roared, waving his heavy stick. He struck the girl a vicious blow. "Disobeying me then you've been, is it? Warned you long ago I did," he yelled as he struck her again. She cried out in pain. "Not this boy again to see, I told you!" He turned on Geraint in fury. "Not to disobey me you are too, I said." Mawddach's heavy beard shook. His jaw quivered with rage. He was about to strike Alwena again when Geraint flew at him.

"Don't you dare strike her again!" he warned, "or

me to answer you'll have to!"

"Insolent dog!" screamed Mawddach turning to threaten him with the stick. "Heavily pay for that you will! Call me 'Chief' with respect as well, you will! On your knees, go!" As he advanced, Geraint side-stepped smartly and struck him a blow to the face with a stone in his hand. Blood flowed from the leader's cheek and, as he dropped his stick, Geraint flew at him again.

Mawddach was incensed. "Pegged out to die for this you'll be!" he bellowed and although the nephew knew he meant it, he had no fear. It was the understood punishment in the tribe for anyone assaulting the leader in that way and there'd be no possible remission for him now. That wasn't what Mawddach had planned for the boy. He'd wanted that complete submission which he'd failed to obtain from his father and, just as he believed he was getting it, his uncontrolled fury had demanded the ultimate punishment.

"Dare, you wouldn't!" challenged Geraint courageously. He pointed to his left shoulder as his uncle attempted to grapple with him again.

"Not save you, that will!" He indicated his own shoulder. "Supreme power over everyone this branch gives me like I told your father!"

Fortunately, they'd been in an isolated spot and Geraint struck him yet another vicious blow which floored him. "Now do what you can!" he challenged, "but catch me first, you'll have to! One day I'll be back avenging you for having had Tad killed! Better watch out you had then for chief I'll be of the tribe and much better than you I'll rule it!"

He grabbed Alwena's hand and they ran with speed before his winded, aggressive relative could prevent them.

"Suffer for this, you will!" cried Mawddach venomously as he youngsters fled.

"I'll never rest now until he's received his full punishment," he informed Alwena as they hurried along.

They had nowhere to go except Deceangli territory and, although the two tribes were at war again, he hoped to receive Iorwerth's protection.

CHAPTER
VI

Mawddach realised their only means of escape was into Deceangli territory and, desperately wanting to prevent Berwyn Goch protecting them, he raced in that direction with a large body of men hoping to overtake them while still on his tribal land. It had taken some time to summon an adequate number to chase them so the young couple had made a considerable start. Regardless, the Ordovician chief was secretly relishing the prospect of a further encounter with his arch enemy if they had already left his territory and entered the adjoining one. Apart from anticipating such action, he spitefully intended to severely punish any of his own people who'd joined the Mynydd Rebels should he come across them.

When he'd mustered his warriors, the sun was already sinking and they had little time to find the trail before nightfall. Nevertheless, he was trusting his hound to solve the problem. He'd given it Geraint's meagre bedding to smell and the animal became excited and eagerly charged after him. It went at such a speed that Mawddach and the able-bodied followers were soon exhausted. When they were forced to pause for a break it annoyed their leader and his vile temper broke forth. "No time to stop, there is," he wheezed breathlessly. " Keep moving!"

The dog wasn't content with the delay and as soon as its master relaxed his grip on its tether it eagerly bounded forward, pulling the chief over and releasing the leash. The hound was away at a tremendous speed, its freed leash trailing.

Repeatedly Geraint and Alwena had changed direction in the hope of confusing their pursuers and surprisingly came across Peris the druid. "Where are you two going in such haste?" he asked with concern.

"From Mawddach Du, we're fleeing," offered Geraint. "Beating Alwena with a stick he's been and hit him, I did."

The druid was amazed. "Hit your tribal chief?" Knowing the severity of the penalty doled out for such an act, he became very concerned.

"Yes, the ultimate penalty on me he's passed regardless of my status – and what to Alwena he'll do if he catches us I don't know but I'll make sure he doesn't achieve that. One day I'll get even with him then chief in his place I'll be." There was no conceit in his statement.

Peris was sympathetic. "The ultimate punishment can only be meted out to ordinary tribesmen, and privileged you are."

"True that is, but so powerful now he thinks he is

that his own rules he breaks." The priest realised the boy was speaking the truth. "Can't stop longer now," he apologized. "Following us he'll be," he stated as they hurried on.

"In peace go, and safely!" the druid called after them.

As dusk turned to night they came upon an empty animal compound. It was composed of substantial interlaced branches to keep out marauding predators. The entrance was vulnerable and, although both were extremely weary, they ignored the repulsive smell and prepared to secure the exposed portion before they rested. When satisfied with the result they considered it to be safe for the night and settled down reasonably well. Before dawn, they were grateful to have spent sufficient time over the preparation. It was a pitch-black night and both had been roused by an old wolf scratching and searching for food. Although somewhat weakened in its ravenous state it was still extremely dangerous. It had obviously been attracted by the lingering animal smell and, after unsuccessfully struggling to find a way in at the reinforced entrance, it had prowled around seeking for any weakness in the fence. The ordeal was far from pleasant, for the two had no real means of defending themselves.

They listened to its persistent assaults with mounting trepidation, uncertain what action to take. Despite all their shouting it made no difference to the wolf. Suddenly the sound of its efforts was quietened by a ferocious growl which terminated in a tremendous fight. Due to the restriction of the visibility they were uncertain what was happening. The indistinct shadowy bodies moving about in the sombre darkness completely confused them. The noise of the savagely contested fight reached a crescendo before it faded out. Although still puzzled they had to wait for dawn before they solved the mystery. They then discovered the wolf dead and to their surprise some distance away lay Mawddach's wolfhound. The dog had been so severely mauled it was too weak even to whimper and merely pleaded for assistance through pathetic looking eyes.

Picking up Geraint's scent again after jerking free of its cruel master it had traced them to the enclosure in time to save them from the wolf. Soon after daybreak Geraint found a nearby pool where he bathed the dog's wounds before gently binding them with fronds. He gave it a drink and the animal feebly expressed its thanks through worshipping eyes. They made it as comfortable as possible by screening it against the rising sun in a small semi secluded spot behind a large oak tree.

"Sorry to have to leave you friend," said Geraint dolefully, stroking it with affection. "Not caught we must be, and too weak to travel with us you are." The hound issued a very low whine as if he understood, and

Geraint felt terrible at leaving him when he saw the pleading expression in his eyes. He was sure the animal sensed it was being deserted.

As they were nearing Deceangli territory they were suddenly surrounded by hostile tribesmen who suspected that the youngsters had been reconnoitring the area as a prelude to a surprise attack. All Geraint's attempts to convince them otherwise had no effect so he suggested that they take them to Iorwerth who he was sure would vouch for them.

Arriving at the Deceangli camp they were taken to Iorwerth and the youngsters instantly experienced disappointment. "Know me, Iorwerth, don't you?" he pleaded. "Tell them not spies we are!" Iorwerth could certainly see the resemblance in the developing beard and moustache, for the boy so clearly resembled Hywel, but not knowing his motive he was uncertain whether he could trust him. "How do I know you, or can trust you?" he questioned. "Often alongside that villainous Mawddach Du when warring against us you've been and no son of Hywel would subscribe to such betrayal."

"But not changed I have," he pleaded.

"Wouldn't have helped that wicked leader if not changed you have! Your memory of such a dear father wouldn't have permitted it."

"Look, Geraint I am." He revealed the crow on his left shoulder.

"No disputing that there is – but not fit to wear

such an emblem now you are!" Iorwerth spat out his contempt. "Changed you have from the decent, dedicated little boy you were some years ago. Devious as that repulsive uncle you seem to have become now, so why should I believe you? You're certainly no longer a baby so must have had many opportunities to escape from that murderous villain yet you stayed! You come here now pretending you mean no harm when you've obviously supported his actions in attacking us by being alongside him as you were. You're no credit to your father's memory and I don't know what he'd think of you if he saw you now."

"Made me go with him he did – really!"

"Not telling the truth you are! He's sent you here, it's one of his many devious tricks and you're already part of his wicked scheme."

"No, Iorwerth! Not, I am. Forced me to go with him always he did – honest!" Becoming increasingly desperate he looked appealingly at Iorwerth but only saw cold disgust, and his hopes crumbled.

"Rubbish!" snarled the banished Ordovician. "Here, with lies from that wicked uncle, you've come!" Geraint's hopes were instantly shattered. Never for a moment had he expected Iorwerth to doubt him. "Not the defenceless pleading eight-year-old I left, you are now. Do you expect me to believe it's taken you a full eight years to leave him? Nonsense that is!"

"Chances I had but wanted to be big enough to

repay him for Tad, so waited I did. Would have waited a bit longer but made me hit him, he did. Responsible for Tad's brutal death he was I'm sure, and that I'll never forget. He set the Romans on his own brother and had him killed. A proper vile beast he is!"

"Don't you dare refer to your late respected father as if you had feeling for him! A man of great integrity Hywel was. He was worth knowing – and that you'll never be!"

Geraint gasped. There was a lump in his throat which threatened to choke him. Iorwerth's statement was a severe stab in the back – something he'd never expected. He'd wanted help and consideration from the man he'd always admired, trusted, and held in such great esteem since childhood. Despite his present attitude the young man still retained a strong respect for him, but the hurt became more pronounced as he realised his precarious position.

"You should never have bowed to that bullying uncle of yours like you have, whatever the circumstances," continued Iorwerth bitterly. "Big enough to decide for yourself for years now you've been, yet nothing you did! You've become as underhanded as that Mawddach himself and under those circumstances help you I won't. Let Berwyn Goch decide your fate when he returns, I will."

"Iorwerth!" he pleaded desperately, but it had no effect.

As his father's former lieutenant turned his back and was striding away Geraint's expectations were plunged into the depth of despair, for as he departed the youngsters were seized and roughly bundled into a dingy well-guarded hut.

"Now what to do are we?" questioned a terrified Alwena. "The idea of yours it was to come to Iorwerth – and look how he's treated us!" Her annoyance was clearly displayed. "Not have listened to you, I should! What with us will they do now?"

"I don't know." Geraint, miserably considering the impossibility of escape, said nothing more.

"No answer then you've got? Better to have stayed with Mawddach's punishment it would be than be here like this!" she snarled. "Hate you, I do!" she declared viciously. "With you I shouldn't have come!"

Their prison was not very substantial and even if they had been able to escape there was nowhere for them to go. Assuming they could possibly have avoided the Deceanglis they'd probably have fallen foul of Mawddach who'd have been delighted to exact his painful revenge. Even if they avoided both, there was still the risk of falling into Roman hands.

When the surly guardsman, accompanied by an escort of two powerful tribesmen, came in with a weak, watery soup Geraint challenged him. "What are they going to do with us?" he enquired anxiously.

"Soon enough that you'll see," replied the

unfriendly Deceangli. "See you himself Berwyn will when he arrives," he smirked.

"That will be how long?"

"No concern of yours that is! Wait and see you'll have to!"

Geraint found the answers distressing and they had to wait until the following day before they were presented to him. When roughly dragged before Berwyn, the sixteen-year-old, like his father previously, was shocked at his size. Having already harboured vague memories of him being big at the time he'd been offered as an eight-year-old hostage, he thought his imagination could have been playing him false. Now, although almost fully grown he was amazed how insignificant he felt beside him and increasingly marvelled that his father had been able to subdue him.

"Son of my late friend Hywel you say you are!" he bawled out in rage, "yet to spy on us you've come!"

"Not spies we are," insisted Geraint resolutely, hoping it would ensure their freedom.

"From that treacherous Mawddach Du to spy on us you've come, Iorwerth thinks," the Deceangli chief persisted.

"Escaping from him we are. Hit him I did and the ultimate penalty he's sentenced me to. To seek your protection we are here."

Berwyn's guffaw reverberated around the

compound. "Hit Mawddach Du you say? Rubbish!"

"Hit him I did."

Berwyn's laughter ceased instantly. His scowl darkened. "LIES, you tell me," he spat. "Murder a young lad like you for that Mawddach would!"

"Hit him I did," insisted Geraint. "With a big stick he attacked Alwena here and that I wouldn't let him get away with!"

"Believe that, you want me to? Well I won't! Bad as that wicked uncle you are! Using you to come to me with such lies because friend to your father I was. Not get his ultimate penalty you will now – but mine you will!" Berwyn Goch's threat was most dangerous.

"B-ut…"

"No say here you have!" he roared in fury. "Take them away!"

As the guards were firmly seizing them, all were disturbed by an unexpected commotion ending in a piercing outcry. "To see Berwyn Goch right now!" came the demand.

The Deceangli chief was outraged. "Who to disturb me comes here?" he bellowed as Peris the druid forced himself forward in desperation. His mission was so important that the elderly man had managed to wrench himself free from his sturdy retainers.

"Those two release now," he shouted. "I insist!"

"Trouble making to come here like this are you Druid?"

"No. In peace I come!"

"Peace? Peace? When a noise like that you make! Only because a druid you are has saved you or run through I'd have had you!"

Knowing he was safe, the sage persisted. "Protect them you must Berwyn Goch. Mawddach Du is chasing them, so back to their own tribe they dare not go. In Hywel's memory you owe it to them! Spared you when killed you he could didn't he?"

"If lies you tell me, Druid, all members of the Gorsedd to save you, won't help!" He turned to the tribesmen holding the youngsters. "Let them go, but careful eyes keep on them!" He paused. "No. To Iorwerth take them. Make sure no mischief they do, he will."

CHAPTER
VII

The following morning Iorwerth collected Geraint. "Under my care now you are," he announced. "No treachery of any kind from you I'll allow. If anything I suspect, no mercy at all I'll show you." He couldn't have been clearer.

"Depend on me Iorwerth really you can."

"For your sake, I hope you're right. You're coming with the Mynydd Rebels and you'll be watched all the time. We believe those beastly Romans are creating problems around Tryfan so we're going to investigate there."

"Far into Ordovice territory that is," stated Geraint with concern. "Risk of Mawddach seeing us and problems that will cause."

"Pretending to be frightened then you are, is it?"

"No. Significant risk for all it will be on Mawddach's land. If you he finds too, then double success he'll have." He was desperately trying to warn Iorwerth.

"To fight your own tribesmen, you are prepared then?"

"Yes, if us they fight!" Geraint was amazed at his answer. "My loyalty to the Ordovices long ago ceased," he stated. Iorwerth certainly had no intention of fighting his own people if it could possibly be avoided but didn't divulge that to the youngster. He specially mentioned the area referred to, knowing it would be a tremendous risk, particularly since it was not that far from Mawddach's own compound of Llyn Llydaw. It had been done to test his reaction. He believed that if the boy still had affiliation with his uncle it would be a good way to expose him. As a special precaution, he'd charged every Rebel to carefully watch the lad's movements. "Pretending to be frightened of coming against your uncle now, are you? Or are you hoping to betray us?"

"No, Iorwerth, I'm not! Worried I am that he could catch you. Never forgets or forgives as you well know does that horrible uncle of mine!"

"Oh, consideration for me is it now?" Iorwerth's tone was very sarcastic.

"Yes," he replied truthfully.

"Didn't think of that when beside your wicked leader, you fought against us, did you?" Something about it then you could have done, couldn't you, but didn't?" Watching carefully, he registered the disappointment and horror on the young Cadwaladr face. "Watched most closely you'll be," he said fiercely, "and at the first false move, no mercy you'll get!" Geraint was greatly upset to realise Iorwerth didn't trust him and just as he was about to appeal further they were ordered to move off. "A long way to go there is, so no time to waste we've got," stated Iorwerth. "Keep out of Ordovices' way and beware of Romans too! Much progress to make there is and not in a day we'll do it – so move!"

They'd proceeded some distance at a pace when Alwena caught up with them. She was completely breathless. Iorwerth was livid. "What doing here, you are?" he demanded harshly.

"Coming with you, I am," she stated.

"Not you are! Man's business this is! No place for females! Back at once, go!"

"With Geraint staying I am," she announced determinedly, then turned on Geraint in rage.

"One of us you said he was!"

"He is but…"

"…Another of your horrid little tricks, again is it?" demanded Iorwerth in anger. "Encouraged her to follow us so she can rush off and inform Mawddach Du, is it? Let you off and a sizeable reward for your treachery he'd give you?" His tone was most sarcastic. "All his diabolical traits he's certainly taught you, I see!"

"No idea I had she was following," protested Geraint.

"Lies again it is!" His eyes bored into him. "Well back right away she's going – or worse for you it'll be!"

"Go back at once Alwena," commanded Geraint roughly. Although hurting her, he knew he had no choice. "You shouldn't really have come!"

"With you I want to be, so I won't go!"

"Go back!" he yelled, "or hit you I will!" The instant he'd bawled at her he regretted it. He'd never been so cruel to her before but the situation was confusing. "They'll not hurt you there – and if they do they'll have me to answer to."

"Not going, I said – and hate you Geraint Cadwaladr I do!" Her verbal onslaught was completely unexpected and as her boy moved forward to fulfil his threat, Iorwerth restrained him.

"Guards!" he called impatiently and immediately two robust Deceanglis appeared. "Out of my sight take this girl. Have her locked up at the camp and don't let her follow us again!" As the group set off once more Alwena was forcibly returned to her hut kicking and screaming. In desperation, she inflicted a severe scratch on the arm of one of her escorts who gave her a stinging blow across the face before dashing off to stench the flow of blood. As soon as his back was turned Alwena quickly picked up a rock and knocked the remaining guard unconscious before chasing after the rapidly moving Rebels again. Her action had been so quick that she was on her way before being missed at the camp.

The Mynydd Rebels moved fast but Alwena also moved rapidly in her determination to catch them up. The Rebels had taken a circuitous southerly direction to cross the Conwy at a shallower part of the river, hoping to avoid both Mawddach and the Romans.

Alwena, having anticipated their caution, made off on a more easterly course. Hastily plunging into the river at the nearest point she immediately regretted it. The icy, fast-flowing water tore the breath from her body. The river was much colder than she'd expected and it also shelved steeply. Up to her neck within seconds she frenziedly struck out. Although a reasonably strong swimmer, the going wasn't easy. She'd confronted a strong, ebbing tide which edged her in the direction of the river mouth as she attempted to plough her way across. Her wet clothes severely hampered her attempts to reach the farther bank. When she did arrive there, she flopped on to a small grassy bank to relieve her aches and was soon lying in a pool of dripping water. She was furious to find herself much further north than she'd expected, yet in a semi exhausted state she felt it was impossible to move for some time. Fortunately, the sun was reasonably high but it had insufficient strength to counter the chilly wind which caused her to shiver. She lay for some time regaining her breath despite being extremely aware of her urgent desire to catch up with the Mynydd Rebels.

When a threatening cloud covered the sun and the chill wind increased she was forced to act. Directing her course slightly south easterly she was aware of further difficulties. She needed exceptional luck to find the Rebels before being confronted by Mawddach's men as she'd expect no sympathy from the latter. Every time she came in sight of higher ground she forced herself to climb to the top to scan the surrounding landscape in the hope of seeing Iorwerth's group, but she was unsuccessful. Constant climbs and descents in the hope of achieving her objective soon took their toll. She became extremely weary again and reluctantly had to rest. Lying down in a small meadow she was unable to keep her eyes open and fell into a deep slumber. She was awakened with a start by a warm breath fanning her face. It took her several seconds to remember the location and heaving herself up in terror, realised she'd been roused by Mawddach's hound. Relief and gratitude engulfed her and she wrapped her arms around it and hugged it with delight.

"Found me out here have you?" she exclaimed, gripping it even tighter. The animal seemed equally pleased to see her, as it licked her face with delight. Alwena was saddened to see the horrible scars caused by the wolf's mauling. The dog was anything but fully recovered, yet its presence gave her immense pleasure as she continued her search.

A little later she caught sight of Peris and regretted he was too far away to reach. She wanted to know if he'd seen anything of the Mynydd Rebels. As she watched, Peris seemed utterly blasé about his safety and it worried her. Having always believed his position would save him, he now seemed to be taking a risk by heading towards the coast regardless of any possible danger. Alwena was concerned that he could seriously imperil himself if accosted by the disrespectful Romans who cared nothing for his position. They had already been extremely brutal to several of his calling and seemed determined to attack everybody whenever they had the chance. The invaders considered him and those like him a menace and wrongly accused them of being the focal point of the insurgencies. Some had been beaten to death for suspected involvements but Peris, as usual, was fearless. He considered his status would always safeguard him.

Sometime later the hound became excited. Having constantly sniffed the ground, it impatiently dashed forward for a short spell before returning to Alwena as if imploring her to hurry. Rightly suspecting it could have picked up Geraint's scent she hastened after it and following its lead she eventually spotted a group travelling at speed, and from the animal's excited bark she was certain it was those she wanted. On getting closer, the animal bounded away to greet Geraint who was equally pleased to see it.

"That fearsome looking beast's Mawddach's isn't it?" snarled Iorwerth suspiciously, noting the attention it gave to Geraint.

"Yes, but while it's with me it won't hurt anyone if left alone."

"But Mawddach he'll lead us to, won't he?"

"No. Totally deserted him now, it has. Years of heartless treatment from him he had. So, to me he belongs and not to that beastly uncle I have to settle with it will lead us."

Iorwerth's suspicions regarding Geraint were increasing greatly and he became determined to watch him even more.

CHAPTER
VIII

Mawddach, searching for Geraint with a small party of tribesmen had spotted the Mynydd Rebels in the distance but realising that their force was more powerful than his own, cowardly he avoided engaging them. The confidence he'd placed in the sneaky Tyddyn Fach's ability to snoop hadn't been misplaced. The informer, having discreetly followed them, had hurried back to report all the information he'd gleaned.

"To Tryfan they're coming. For the Romans, trouble they want to make." The Ordovice chief was delighted. "Trouble for them there will be if the Romans we tell soon enough." Mawddach was enthralled. Nothing could have suited him better. Instantly he left off trailing them and, rubbing his hands with glee, he made for the nearest Roman Hill Fort. To prevent any misunderstanding, he deposited his followers in a thick copse at the base of the hill. They were well out of sight when he commenced the ascent alone, with extreme care, for he'd never actually been to that Hill Fort before.

"With Flavius to speak, I want," he told the guard.

"He's not here," stated the approaching legionnaire

who'd heard what he'd said.

"The Mynydd Rebels he wants, isn't it?" enquired the Celt of the guard who'd kept him waiting at the gate.

"What sort of horrible trick is this?" demanded the fort's second-in-command with unreserved suspicion.

"No trick it is," stated Mawddach somewhat concerned. He'd expected the type of warm welcome he received at the Hill Fort he normally visited but it didn't seem to be forthcoming. "Towards Tryfan going they are. Trouble for you there to make, isn't it?"

"Don't you dare come here with false tales!" roared the legionnaire drawing his sword threateningly, making Mawddach wonder if he'd done the right thing after all.

"Wait!" commanded a voice as footsteps approached. A centurion witnessing the scene had recognised Mawddach. "Put that sword away," he instructed. "This is the one who led Flavius to that rascally trouble maker years ago. We may as well hear what he has to say, it could be useful to us." He turned on the Ordovice chief. "I'll have no pity on you if you play us false, you know!" He took Mawddach into the Fort and demanded the full details.

Mawddach could only give him the barest outline as he wasn't in possession of the full details. "By two big oak trees near Penlan to trap them will be the place," he suggested. "There's a large wood nearby where you could hide."

The wily centurion was hurriedly assessing the situation, for he knew exactly where those oaks were situated as he'd regularly passed along that route. Quickly recalling the area, and considering it a very reasonable possibility, he mentally accepted Mawddach's information. He realised that they could use a similar device to that which Flavius was involved in, but this intended plan would have to be more subtle. "Keep this one here until we check out his story and know it's not something to deceive us." The centurion, determined to enhance his reputation with a defeat of the pestering Mynydd Rebels, considered the possibility perfect but he wanted to be sure.

Mawddach was shunted into a hut and carefully guarded.

As time went by his tribesmen waiting in the copse below became restless. All of them were concerned for the safety of their chief but the more timorous Tyddyn Fach, being far more worried for himself as usual, was the first to show concern. "Wrong up there things have gone perhaps," he stated worriedly. "Back by now the chief should be, if all things are right!" In normal circumstances he'd have sneaked up himself to assess the situation, but he considered the risk far too great even for him. "Back by now he should be," he repeated. "Holding him as hostage they must be, I think!"

Concealed in the undergrowth, he stared fixedly at the Fort and on noticing movement decided it was time to go. He'd seen a large contingent preparing to march from the garrison and he had no intention of hanging around to be captured. "Going, I am," he said, "before the Romans find us here. Go yourselves too you must, but not all together like, or be chased you will!" Ensuring his own safety, he made off in haste.

The consensus was with him and, following his lead, they went out in twos and threes to prevent being spotted, but Tyddyn was well away before any of them had had time to move.

Their chief had taken a significant risk but Tyddyn's loyalty didn't extend to being captured for anybody – not even for Mawddach.

CHAPTER

IX

Alwena increased her speed dramatically and eventually caught up with the Rebels again. Iorwerth was furious when she appeared. "A thrashing you deserve!" he bawled the moment he spotted her. "Get back again and take that blasted hound too!"

"I won't," she stated defiantly. "Hard enough finding you it's been, so staying I am! Important news for you I've got too!" Her voice carried a note of concern.

"What, then?" enquired Iorwerth, though without much interest.

"Peris some time ago I saw. Heading for the coast he was. Great danger he could be in there. Too far away for me to catch him he was, but the Romans might see him and capture him. I know not what they'd do with him if they did!"

"No business of yours that's been. Go back now or punish you I will!" As he approached her the hound showed its teeth in defence of Alwena. "Take that horrible animal with you too before I put a sword into it!"

"Not touch that dog you will!" screamed Geraint.

"You I'll have flogged too!" Iorwerth yelled.

"I'll go," offered Alwena, not wanting the boy to suffer. She fell behind, but continued to tag on unobserved at a distance. Being too terrified to go back and face the tribesmen she'd injured, she needed Geraint's presence and protection.

As the sun started to sink, the Rebels were almost within sight of the two oak trees and Alwena, concerned that they could have missed what she'd seen, dashed back to them in an increased state of alarm. "Look there!" she called anxiously. "Peris it is! Being beaten by that massive Roman too!"

As Iorwerth looked, he saw a figure in druid's attire lying on the ground a long way below him. Apparently, a Roman soldier was thrashing him with a stick and the victim's weak, agonised cries reached him. As he watched, the Roman pounding the body seemed satisfied that he'd done enough and appeared to stride off leaving the cloaked figure motionless on the ground with feeble pathetic groans continuing to come from him.

Geraint, having seen what had happened, cried out. "Fiend! To a man of peace doing that! Peris doesn't deserve it, he's never hurt anybody! Coming to help you Peris, I am." As he started to move Iorwerth grabbed his arm impulsively.

"If this isn't a trap that you're a party to, then grave danger you could be in. Go myself, I will."

"Not twice would they use that trick," the boy cried as his father's demise came flooding back and the memory caused him intense anger. He shook himself free but Iorwerth grabbed his tunic.

"Not going you are!" Iowerth said with authority. "Trapped like that your father was, so what if another deceitful ploy of Mawddach this is? Using the pair of you to snare us like this, he could be. Determined to stick with us this girl has been, and quick to see the situation too she was. In a big hurry to lead us down there you were as well!"

"Going myself I was until you stopped me!"

"Want me to believe that? Well, we'll wait a little while and then I'll go myself. The Rebels won't risk being ambushed to please you or anybody else! Besides, if it's a trick, there's a better chance of my getting away on my own."

That seemed to make sense, as Iorwerth was renowned for his agility. Ensuring that both Geraint and Alwena were firmly held, he made a cautious approach towards the prostrate figure while the remaining Rebels watched anxiously. On nearing the cloaked figure, he quickly realised his mistake. The body was far too big and powerful looking to have been the elderly druid. "Get away quick!" he yelled at his men as he turned to run. Several Romans poured out of the copse the moment they realised Iorwerth had discovered their deception. However, he'd made a reasonable start and their carefully aimed javelins fell short.

Geraint seized the opportunity. "Run," he hissed to Alwena and both managed to get away before the Rebels, recovering from the shock of their narrow escape, had been able to stop them.

"You'll pay for this Geraint Cadwaladr," yelled the maddened Rebel leader, noticing the two youngsters evading the rest of the group as they fled. He still had strong suspicions that in some way they'd been involved and was determined to allow them no mercy if he ever caught up with them again.

The youngsters had a good start on the Rebels who'd been more concerned with Iorwerth's safety than preventing their escape. Geraint was amazed that his father's former lieutenant had almost been caught in the trap. But he'd used the situation to his advantage. Both had run madly using every bit of cover to improve their chances. They'd swerved and dodged repeatedly until they were certain they'd lost their pursuers, and even then they didn't falter. As darkness descended they holed up in a dense wood and anxiously discussed their predicament as they now had so many enemies to avoid. It was dangerous for them to remain in Ordovice country as Mawddach would have no mercy if they were discovered there. A similar situation would arise from Berwyn Goch as now Iorwerth would undoubtedly be hunting them down. If they managed to evade both there remained the Romans to be very concerned about, for the brutal intruders made slaves of any natives they caught.

"Go where then, can we?" enquired Alwena desperately when the difficulties had been spelled out. "The dog to think of too there is. Fortunately, it's not given us away yet, but would if by any of the tribes it was spotted. Geraint had been wracking his brain for a course of action, having already appreciated that the hound could become a massive problem. To keep it could lead the pursuers to them, and any attempt to turn it away would have no guarantee for it possibly would have trailed them. "To get to Deva is the best thing to try," he mused aloud. "Celts are already inside that fortress, they say, and we could possibly pass ourselves off as Roman sympathisers if we're careful.

"Deva? Deva? Where that is?"

"Well, Caer we call it."

"Caer?" she yelled. "Mad you must be Geraint Cadwaladr. To go into that Roman Fortress dangerous it is. It would be impossible with the dog too!"

"The risk could be great," he admitted, "but nobody would know us there and nowhere else to think of, is there? We just can't stay out here for ever you know!"

"Alone you'll have to go then," she stated firmly and his heart sank, for he hadn't expected that type of opposition from her. "I'll not risk being discovered there. Bad enough the Romans are out here, crueller in Deva they could be!"

"Not if very careful we are. Not only soldiers are there but civilians too."

"Careful, you say! A lot of luck we'd need too!" Alwena was clearly not prepared to take the risk and firmly expressed her objection.

"Nowhere else to go there is and not leaving you, I am. A better chance together we'll have." He was showing his strong concern.

"Know that I do. There are too many dangers for me if left on my own I am, and that I don't want." Alwena's tears were evident.

"What suggest you then?" He was trying to be helpful.

"What to do I don't know. To the coast, we can go, I suppose."

"More risk from the Romans down there, there'll be."

"Still, not have heard of us there perhaps those people will, so better it will be," she repeated.

"Well, make up our minds we've got to!" Geraint's irritation was growing.

"I know that!"

"Knowing that and doing nothing is no good. If you don't make up your mind I'm off – so what's it to be?" He was forcing her hand.

"To the coast go, I say!"

Geraint didn't like her taking the initiative but he

was determined not to leave her, so he finally gave way and they moved, knowing they had to be extremely careful.

Cautiously heading in a north easterly direction, hours later they were within reach of Llyn Cowlyn where they rested. Both were very hungry and after a brief pause came to a dwelling near the lake which, after a careful inspection, revealed nobody was at home. On entering they found some hard-baked black bread and some cold mutton. Tearing off chunks of the bread they were just about to start on the mutton when a gravelly voice disturbed them.

"Doing what, here you are?" demanded an old man with a husky voice, who glared at them. "Stealing, is it?" The dog growled, showing its dislike of the frail-looking old man. Geraint was forced to grab it and pull it to heel by the scruff of the neck. "Where from you've come?" demanded the ageing Delyn.

"Mona," lied Geraint instantly to put him off. He'd been surprised at own swift response. "Escaping from the Romans we are and a long way we've come without food,"

"Not Ordovices then you are?"

"Well Ordovices we really are," he stated, expecting him to be one of the tribe and hoping the old man hadn't learned they were being chased.

"No trouble from those Romans here there will be. Too far from their hill forts it is. Take sheep from other herdsmen down the valley they do but not this far they come. Nearer to them down there they are." The old man was studying them carefully through screwed up eyes. "Work to pay for your food you'll have to. Round up my sheep for me – but go that dog must! With wolves, enough trouble I've had as it is!"

"This hound's not frightened of wolves. Killed one some days ago, he did."

"Keep it then, you might. On a string put it, for not my sheep to touch, it is!"

"How many sheep have you got?" Geraint was stalling, rapidly trying to decide what to do.

"Forty. Scattered across that hillside too they are. Not easy to catch and too much for me they're getting, but feed me they must."

Geraint would have liked to have discussed the matter with Alwena but that could have raised the old man's suspicions. As he turned towards the girl he noticed a sly nod of approval and decided to accept, for they really had no alternative.

The old man wanted the sheep rounded up and brought to an area nearer his dwelling. He promised them something to eat upon their return. With the dog leashed the two set off on the mission anticipating the enjoyment of a much-needed meal. The scattered flock, frightened by the dog's appearance proved difficult to round up and it took them well into the evening to achieve their objective. The ordeal had taken quite a lot out of them and they became totally ravenous. Having just received a welcome bowl of mutton soup they were all disturbed by a cacophony of worried bleating from the sheep outside and the old man went out to investigate.

"Roman soldiers coming, isn't it?" he announced with a note of concern.

Quick as a flash, Geraint poured the two bowls of soup back into the pan and both the youngsters hurriedly concealed themselves beneath a heap of smelly old sheep fleece, which the resident seemed to use as a bed, in the darkest corner of old Delyn's hut. Geraint successfully muzzled the dog with his hands.

"Had any strange people around here?" demanded the leading Roman.

"Nobody to this place comes," stated Delyn hoping he wouldn't discover the youngsters. "The first see, you are!"

The soldier took a sniff. "Ah, food I smell, as well as something vile." He pushed himself inside. "Food is what I need so I'll put up with the horrible smell." The dog uttered a low growl as it tried to get up to see what was happening. Fortunately, the Roman thumped the table at that moment and the animal wasn't heard. "Food, I want!" he bellowed demandingly and Geraint was pleased to realise his outburst had concealed the hound's second attempted snarl.

The intruder greedily devoured the stew and

instantly demanded more, which he ate with equal speed. Fortunately, he had no consideration for the wants of the others with him. "Too much stew for one man that was," he declared with a note of suspicion.

"All week for me to live on that had to be," offered Delyn. "Every day too much work for me to make a meal there is and nothing left I've got now!"

The Roman was callous. "You'll have to starve for a week then, won't you!" His cruel delight was obvious. If I had my way all you damned Celts would starve for ever! Anyway, you seem to have too many sheep here for an old man like you, so we'll take a few back with us!" Delyn was near to tears over the potential loss. He was silently raging but daren't object in case they took the entire flock. With a vulgar belch the soldier went out. "We've wasted too much time here so we might as well have something for our trouble. Slaughter four sheep, and we'll take them back with us."

As the cries of the disturbed sheep seemed to penetrate the area the hound broke loose and flew at the intruder. The Roman's reaction was swift. He gave the dog a terrific kick which sent it limping away with an instinct not to return to Geraint.

"We now know where to come when we want more sheep," threatened the stern faced Roman. I know where to come when I want more stew too – so you'd better have it ready and if that dammed dog comes near me again it'll be the last thing it ever does!"

Geraint was afraid that there would be a tremendous risk to the old man as well as themselves if they stayed as it would have been impossible to conceal themselves a second time. Apart from that the Roman had eaten all the stew.

Delyn was disappointed when Geraint announced the decision, as he'd hoped the youngsters could have been useful with his sheep. Nevertheless he understood their position. He couldn't understand what they'd have done to be chased by the Romans but didn't want them discovered with him as it would have caused extreme danger.

Before they left, Delyn generously gave them some dark bread and a little cold mutton even though it depleted his own limited supply.

They set off blindly in the starlit night with no idea as to where they were heading. Their main objective was to distance themselves from that place in case the Romans returned. They hugged the course of the Afon as it flowed from Llyn Cowlyn. Having no knowledge of where it would lead, they used it as a rough guide by keeping to the southerly bank.

Early next morning Peris caught up with them and seemed relieved. "Glad to have found you, I am." He seemed genuinely pleased. "Mawddach Du and his tribesmen are all over the place this side of the big river. They're telling everybody to look out for a boy and girl and he's promised a reward for whoever finds them." He turned to Alwena and handed her a large head cover. "Put this on," he suggested. "It will disguise your identity. You need a lot more mud on your face too and you should pretend to be dumb if anyone stops you," he advised. "Must go now before anyone knows I've found you. Take care. Mawddach's a very nasty man and will have no mercy if ever he catches you." Without further comment, he turned sharply and hurried out of sight.

To try to prevent their discovery they progressed very carefully at night concealing themselves whenever they could by day. Progress was naturally slow but when the Afon Ddu ran into the bigger river they stopped to consider the situation. "Safer on the other side it will be since Mawddach's chasing us on this side." Geraint revealed his concern. "Besides there are auxiliary Roman forts at Bryn-y-Gefellium and Caerhun on this side from which they can possibly see us."

"But there's Deceangli territory over there," protested Alwena, viewing the width, depth and flow of the river. It was obvious she didn't fancy crossing at that point.

"Better take that chance than be captured by Mawddach," insisted Geraint. Alwena was not convinced and it took some time to persuade her. "Go north we should," he suggested as they pulled their dripping bodies on to the opposite bank. "We'll risk running into the Deceanglis more if the other way we go."

"But there'd be more Romans to avoid if we went that way!" Alwena revealed she'd rather take her chance with a fearsome tribe that she could communicate with than face the invaders.

"But not only by the Romans we could be being chased, isn't it? We'll have to be careful to avoid them of course but they might take us for a pair of inoffensive youngsters if you play your part properly."

Alwena took even more persuading but eventually they set off along the river bank with extreme caution.

Having successfully followed the river towards its mouth for some distance they came across a herdsman struggling to move four wild, self-willed cattle. The animals were creating chaos by darting in all directions and the elderly herdsman had difficulty in controlling them.

Geraint, seizing his chance, whispered to Alwena to play her part. "Where to, those cattle you're taking?" he enquired.

"A camp near the copper mines on that Craig Mawr which looks to the sea. I hope to sell them to the Romans there."

"Then help you want, isn't it and help you we can, see!" He could see the cowherd looking curiously at Alwena who'd started to act her part by spasmodically jerking her right shoulder as if she were unable to control it. "About my friend here, don't worry. He'll be quite useful." He hoped Alwena now looked more like a boy than a girl. The man seemed satisfied with the assurance and they moved off with him.

Progress had only slightly improved. Even with the three of them herding, the beasts were still difficult enough to control. They wandered left and right as if they were aware of their impending fate and objected to being slaughtered. The three of them were moving reasonably well again after a particularly turbulent session and they had almost got complete control when they were set upon by three fierce looking Deceanglis who viewed Geraint with deep suspicion.

"To handle four cows, three of you it takes, then is it?" scoffed one of the three. "And where do you think you're taking them then?"

"Near the copper mines on Craig Mawr," stated the herdsman with a nervous croak. He was obviously fearing that the unwelcome trio would take his stock.

"Only two of us are any good really," stated Geraint pointing to Alwena who was rapidly twitching her right arm again. "Idiot that one is. No help he is see. These cows have come straight down from the mountain and wild they are see! Not seen a human for months they have and completely unruly they are as you can see."

"Still doesn't take three of you to drive four cattle!" He sounded suspicious.

Geraint held his breath, fearing the cowman might give them away. He wondered if he'd explain that the two were strangers who'd only just joined him. Fortunately, the old man ignored the remark and didn't betray them. He gently let out his breath again and felt a little easier.

"Romans only on the Craig Mawr camp there are," stated the leader with scorn. "Friends of those horrible intruders you are then – and not true Celts like us!"

"Not Roman's friends we are but sell these cows I must. Too much for me to look after they are and their price I need! To fight the Romans these two want."

"Lot of fight in that one there'd be," he scoffed pointing to Alwena. "Traitors you are if these cattle you let our enemies have! Even for thinking of it, killed all three of you should be! Save you the bother though now we will and take them ourselves!"

As soon as they started to round up the restless beasts, one of them called, "Watch out! Coming are six Romans and the look of them I don't like!" The Deceanglis instantly abandoned the cattle and sped off, leaving the three to the mercy of the Romans. One of them mockingly hurled back, "Chance to fight them now, you've got!"

Whether through fear or some other reason the old man had suddenly seemed older and his back seemed to be far more bent.

CHAPTER
X

Shortly after leaving the two young people, Peris heard the hound groaning with pain. Searching carefully, he found it under some thick shrubs. His initial inspection revealed the horrible gash where the Roman's stout sandal had landed. The dog was wheezing badly as if one of its ribs had been shattered.

The creature graciously accepted his soothing words of comfort. The druid gently examined it more closely then bandaged the wound as best he could with his own vestments and made it as comfortable as possible. On seeing it was desperately in need of nourishment, he walked a considerable distance to the nearest hutment and begged some scraps of food. The inhabitants, astounded to find the religious man short of food, quickly produced some and became even more amazed to find that instead of eating it he simply wrapped it in his cloak, thanked them and hurriedly left.

Although the dog was hungry it seemed to have insufficient strength to tackle the food Peris offered it, so the druid patiently encouraged it to take a little at a time. As soon as he'd made it reasonably content again he reluctantly left, intending to return as early as possible. Knowing that the animal had attached itself to the two youngsters, he was surprised not to find them around looking after it. He'd worried over the hound all night and early in the morning he returned to the spot – but he'd been noticed. Iorwerth, with the full complement of Mynydd Rebels had been searching for Geraint so desperately that they'd overlooked nothing and their diligence hadn't waned. They'd noticed the druid dashing with unusual haste and Peris' manner suggested he could have had some mysterious motive. On noting that he was carrying something, Iorwerth's suspicion increased. When he discovered he'd been hurrying to Mawddach's hound he was surprised, then remembered the animal had firmly attached itself to the youths, so hoped it would lead him to Hywel's disgraceful son.

He approached Peris. "What's Mawddach's hound doing here?" he demanded with respect, "and why are you fussing over it like this?"

"What are you doing on Mawddach's land I could ask? To Berwyn's territory you belong now."

"No restriction there is for me, Druid. Like Hywel Cadwaladr, my former leader, I am now. I belong to the whole Celtic nation just like you, and all our people are the same. The entire land is our home and our ambition is to clear it of Roman interference. "Mawddach Du," he spat out the name with a contempt that emphasised his loathing for that person, "an outcast has made me, but I will still roam his territory. Like Hywel, I'm prepared to die trying to stop these Romans." Peris fully understood his commitment and, although a man of peace, he quietly supported Iorwerth's sentiment. "To catch Hywel's son though is my first aim. He's disgraced his father's memory. You must know where he is Druid, so take me to him!"

"No knowledge where he is I've got!" Iorwerth's slight threat annoyed Peris, "And don't you dare threaten me!" he added with a touch of savagery.

"You do know," he insisted disregarding the priest's status.

"Lying, you say I am?" snapped Peris sharply. "A calling of truth and peace mine is!"

Iorwerth still had certain reservations regarding the druid's integrity but, expecting to get nothing further from him, decided to prolong matters no further. However, he would keep very watchful eye on him, hoping to be led to Geraint.

The youngsters had been spotted crossing the Conwy by a legionnaire from Bryn-y-Gefeilium and news had been speedily sent to the Romans at Caerhun which was situated much nearer the mouth of the Afon Conwy. Thus, six legionnaires had been quickly rowed across the river by enslaved Welshmen in order to intercept them.

"Those are stolen animals," accused one legionnaire, cutting them off as his accomplices surrounded both humans and cattle.

"Not they are!" replied Geraint as firmly as he could while noticing the look of apprehension on the owner's face. "To the camp near the copper mines to try to sell them we're going."

"That's an unlikely tale! Still if you're eager to get there, you can come with us. We'll find you something far more worthwhile to do than minding a few straggly cattle." His grin was disturbing.

His colleagues quickly grabbed the two youngsters and having no use for the frail looking old man told him he could go.

Geraint and Alwena were hustled half a mile along the river bank to the vessel which also held other captured Celts. As they went he caught the look of concern on the old man's face and cursed their misfortune. Once aboard the craft they were rowed by their fellow countrymen towards the river mouth. The overseer in charge was constantly cracking his whip to hasten them on.

"Where are you taking us?" Geraint enquired of one of the oarsmen and was instantly struck a stinging blow across his back.

"No talking I'll have!" snapped the Roman in charge and although Geraint's fury mounted he realised he had to restrain himself.

Unceremoniously disembarking on to a small jetty they were forcibly marched at regulation pace as far as the great headland jutting out to sea. The climb up that long steep slope was extremely arduous after their earlier ordeal, yet whenever they slackened their pace they were prodded unmercifully and told to move faster.

Arriving at their destination they were immediately sent into the mine to extract copper ore. Geraint and Alwena were separated and given different tasks but still managed an occasional contact with each other through a code they'd used when younger, for there was a strict ban on conversation and normal communication was difficult. Whenever the two got near each other Geraint wracked his brain to find some word of encouragement and support knowing it was imperative not to let Alwena become depressed.

He'd immediately been set to work on the rock face, strenuously chiselling to extract the mineral. The work was very dusty and backbreaking and the conditions extremely cramped. Pieces of splintered rock flew in all directions causing cuts and bruises to many, but such misfortunes had to be ignored as the enslaved miners were whipped for the slightest pause and made to continue.

Overseers wielding heavy thongs were constantly moving up and down behind them and they showed no sympathy for the injured. One overseer, who from the colour of his skin had obviously originated from North Africa, took fiendish delight in unmercifully whipping anyone who attempted to take the slightest rest, while sweaty and grimy lacerated bared backs were in evidence everywhere. The air continually reeked of human perspiration.

Alwena was employed carrying buckets of the extracted contents to the checking inspector before it was sent to the furnace for smelting. She continued to adopt the pretence of being an idiot to conceal her gender. She periodically tweaked her left shoulder in the hope that her contrived affliction would somehow prove beneficial to them both. On the odd occasion when she'd presented rubble to the checking centurion, although it wasn't strictly her responsibility, she was severely chastised and beaten. The work was strenuous and although she still intimated she had limited use of her arm it brought no relief. She was continuously ordered to carry more and move faster. It all made her wonder if they'd made the right decision in choosing to go towards the coast after all.

Both were kept so constantly occupied that they had little opportunity to see each other and, after several days without sight or contact, Geraint became worried. It would have been disastrous for them both if the Romans had realised she was female and he regularly worried for her safety hoping she wouldn't be discovered. In sheer desperation, to keep in touch, he risked adopting the code they'd used in the copse so many years earlier. At the entrance to the mine he managed to scratch a crude outline of a bird on the right-hand side of the opening without being observed. To his delight, two days later, he saw she'd added a worm to it. He then considered they'd somehow have to risk attempting to meet again. Although it seemed impossible, he felt they'd have to consider any means to try to escape.

It was fortunate that both continued to be reasonably fit considering their labours were so severely punishing. Both cringed when fellow natives, overcome with fatigue, were whipped until they dropped. Although nobody could talk, on the rare occasions when Alwena managed to get close enough to him they risked a sneaky whispered communication.

Despite the work being arduous their cruel taskmasters wouldn't allow them to slow down. The first sign of anyone easing, brought an immediate lash of a whip from the overseers – especially from that coloured North African one. Fortunately, Geraint had been strong enough to be spared humiliation whenever he'd been struck. However, several of his fellow labourers who'd received lashes for unjustifiable reasons had not been able to stand it and, seeing his fellow countrymen being so abused, it took Geraint immense self-control to restrain himself and resist interfering.

Some weeks later things suddenly changed for the worst. Flavius, the centurion who'd been responsible for his father's demise those years earlier, appeared. He'd been given command of the mine and instantly imposed his wicked authority on everyone. When he came across Geraint slogging away as usual, something seemed to click with him but he couldn't determine what it was and it made him so very annoyed. He paused for a while with his eyes boring into him as he tried to recall some previous incident. The youth was now such a perfect likeness of his father that it had registered some chord of recognition in Flavius but he was unable to establish what it was. Nevertheless, he continued to stare, searching for that recognition.

Geraint, conscious of his prolonged presence behind him, felt extremely uncomfortable. He felt certain that this was the beast responsible for his father's dreadful death and chanced to glance behind. Instantly he was rewarded with a resounding blow from the flat of Flavius' stick which caused a nasty bruise.

The Roman, unable to assess him properly in such a dust impregnated atmosphere, called him out towards the entrance to study him more fully. Even then the bullying centurion remained uncertain of whom he reminded him and his annoyance increased. Not being satisfied, he was determined to punish him regardless for raising such a niggling doubt. Everyone had earlier been threatened not to leave their allotted positions for any reason at all so Geraint had been undecided as whether to obey him. Thinking it might have been a ruse merely to bully and humiliate him, he looked around with uncertainty to try to assess whether he should go or not.

Flavius became irate. He prodded Geraint harshly with his stick which caused another severe bruise. "Come here!" he yelled and several faces turned as his command reverberated around the cave. His voice had even, for a few seconds, drowned the perpetual ringing of the hammers which had so constantly been chipping away. "Back to work you lot!" he bawled, brandishing his stick threateningly to ensure he was understood, "or you'll find yourselves at the end of this!"

When Hywel's son approached him in that dark and dusty atmosphere, the warrior, still unable to see him as clearly as he wanted due to the grimy appearance of the youth, was far from satisfied. "You've been told you're never to leave the rock face when you're working, haven't you?" he screamed.

"But called me, you did," offered the boy defensively.

"Nothing of the kind I did," the centurion lied, and to satisfy his sadistic tendency struck him yet another heavy blow. He called to the powerful black overseer. "There's to be double the output from this one from now on – or I'll want to know why!"

"I'll be only too glad to see to that," stated the tyrannical North African with a malicious smile.

Flavius looked even more closely at Geraint. "I'm sure I've come across you somewhere before and when I remember where it was I'll certainly have no mercy!" The statement was clearly menacing, and although he sounded confident, his hateful manner somehow revealed his uncertainty. "I'll not be satisfied until I remember," he warned, "and then I'll know exactly how to deal with you."

"I don't think you have," stated Geraint courageously, knowing that Flavius must have been referring to his father as his likeness to him had now become pronounced.

The Roman flew into a rage and struck him with his fist.

Get even with you one day I will, Geraint promised himself yet again.

"Respect I'll have from you lot!" roared Flavius, "or you'll all receive more strokes! Get back to the face and work!" he commanded Geraint, "and I'll expect a greater output from you all from now on!" He turned to the North African and nodded in Geraint's direction. "Just see that this one works to the limit. Watch him very carefully and really make him suffer if he doesn't produce a great deal more!" He turned to Geraint. "You'll find that was no idle warning I can assure you!" He raised his voice. "I want full respect from all of you too! You've all had it far too easy up to now, so things will change. Anyone creating trouble from now on will be moved to the lead mines at Halkyn and that will be no picnic I can assure you!"

Geraint was tempted to avenge his father's memory by striking back there and then but knew it would serve no purpose. He was at such a disadvantage that there was nothing he could do but accept it. He knew from the expression of hatred on the North African's face that he was in for a tough time and that he'd have to bear it as best he could. There was also Alwena to be considered for there was no knowing what would happen to her without him around. He simply had to be there to protect her if possible. Apart from all that, he realised it would probably lead to unjustified punishments for everybody if he'd been reckless enough to have struck back and he didn't want to inflict even more pain on his already badly treated compatriots.

Gritting his teeth, he became more determined than ever to wreak his revenge on that brutal Flavius and really make him suffer when he did. There was also the problem of the black overseer. He'd have to find a way to settle matters with him too for he'd already started to impose his harsh authority on them all.

CHAPTER
XII

Mawddach was eventually freed by the Romans and was annoyed that his tribesmen were nowhere around. However, when he eventually caught up with his lost people, having berated them for their lack of consideration for him, he continued the search for the escapees, knowing that if they had already crossed into Deceangli land it would be more difficult for him to deal with them; he was eager to prevent Berwyn Goch depriving him of the pleasure of capturing them. Although among his own people, without the protection of his hound he felt somewhat vulnerable. In spite of his bullying attitude he always felt insecure without the dog he so viciously controlled. He also felt let down by Tyddyn Fach. The contemptible little Ordovice had failed him miserably when most needed. He'd expected him to have found the runaways by then, but he hadn't. Despite his renowned guile Tyddyn had been unable to locate either the youngsters or the dog.

"Worthless to me Tyddyn Fach you are!" he bawled when that nosey Ordovice returned to report his lack of success. Tyddyn had quaked. Despite his having induced the tribesmen to scatter from the copse it wasn't the reception he'd anticipated. He was extremely nervous as his chief was renowned for inflicting painful punishments when in such a mood. Having hoped for a sympathetic understanding, the sound of Mawddach's vicious outburst followed him as he made a rapid exit. "Back here you'll come!" shouted Mawddach but the sneaky informer, not prepared to face his wrath, ignored the command and decided to wait for a more favourable opportunity when he hoped to have something worthwhile to report.

Wandering around somewhat uncertainly, Tyddyn chanced to spot Peris at a distance. The priest seemed to be in such an uncharacteristic rush that he considered it could be advantageous to follow him. "Going where in such a hurry you are, Druid?" he enquired on catching him up. He noticed Peris was carrying a small bundle and assumed it could be food for the missing couple. He felt relieved at the prospect of being able to redeem himself in his chief's eyes once he'd discovered their mysterious whereabouts.

"About my business I'm going and no concern of yours that is." The priest had never concealed his strong dislike and mistrust for the wily snooper but the chief's informer considered he had a reasonable chance of being led to his goal if he followed him. Although disappointed with the answer, to prevent raising suspicions he shrugged his shoulders as if to indicate that he wasn't particularly interested. But his mind was working furiously. Although he hurriedly moved off in the opposite direction he had every intention of keeping Peris in sight and was determined to find exactly where he was going.

As a master of deception, he had no difficulty in concealing himself within that fern infested terrain as he followed Peris. Whenever the ferns thinned out he was fortunate enough to find convenient boulders or hillocks to hide behind. Repeatedly the druid stopped and looked back to ensure that he wasn't being followed by the slippery Tyddyn. The Ordovice sneak, still convinced that the priest would lead him to the couple Mawddach wanted, carefully managed to avoid detection and his resolve to keep Peris in sight strengthened greatly as they progressed. Exercising the cunning he'd developed over the years, he continued to follow unobserved until he saw the druid eventually disappear behind a clump of thick shrubs.

Tyddyn waited patiently out of sight while Peris spent a considerable time there and became more convinced that he was attending to Geraint and Alwena. When Peris finally re-emerged, Tyddyn continued to play it safe by hiding until he was well out of sight. Having ensured he'd had sufficient time to be far away, the sneaky little Ordovice continued to exercise his renowned stealth as he went to investigate the mystery within the shrubs. To his amazement, he was greeted by the most unwelcome snarl of the injured animal, which forced him to move back so quickly he almost tripped and fell. The hound, which had never taken to Tyddyn, bared its fangs in a threatening manner.

Although disappointed not to find the couple, he considered that mentioning the animal and its position would present some consolation for his tribal leader and restore something of his own diminished credibility.

Despite its condition, the dog detested Tyddyn's presence so much it bravely attempted an unsuccessful attack on him and the coward, having no desire to be savaged, quickly moved out of its reach. Closely observing the condition of the beast Tyddyn became satisfied that there was little likelihood of it moving very far, so became increasingly convinced that the knowledge of its discovery would provide the hoped-for gratitude from Mawddach. Thus, he looked forward to reporting back and being the instrument of uniting his chief with his hound and trusting to receive a welcome reception.

XIII

Marcia, the centurion's attractive dark-haired daughter, through her father's strong influence, had been appointed Superintendent of the baths at Miledium. It was the most prestigious appointment that any female could have received in the entire area. However, the complex had been badly neglected by Claudia whom she was replacing. On being appointed, Marcia had received strict instructions to restore the baths to some form of respectability as quickly as possible, with Claudia as her assistant, or she would be in serious trouble. The ducts supplying the water were heavily clogged with weeds and the baths themselves were impregnated with grime. Claudia had bitterly resented being demoted and had taken an instant dislike to Marcia.

There were only a couple of decrepit, elderly workers to perform all the strenuous tasks and, despite her numerous repeated threats, there been little improvement in their achievements. All their work continued to be extremely unsatisfactory. To return the baths to something like its original splendour it needed suitable robust labourers and not those incompetent two. Marcia decided to demand assistance from her father, fully expecting no objection from him in helping her to achieve her objective. With similar brutal resolves and ambitions as her father, she was unprepared to sacrifice her new found status and, since all able-bodied males in the area had been carried off to work in the horrible Halkyn lead mine, it left only the two old doddery workers to do as much as they could. That was why it was in such a shocking state.

The hopeful young female had been delighted to receive the appointment but upon taking office she was disappointed to realise the size of the task confronting her. It seemed an impossibility with such a limited workforce. For long she'd harboured a secret hope of finding some virile young man that she could manipulate and flaunt before her friends but had been disappointed to have found none suitable there.

The two feeble old men with which she'd been burdened were nothing like the nice young men she'd envisaged for so long. She'd wanted someone to flirt with and bully in a similar manner to her callous father. That would have satisfied her. Over the years, she'd often derived much pleasure from copying his sadistic behaviour but knew she'd receive no satisfaction in attempting to tyrannise the elderly workers she'd inherited. Judging by their appearance they could quite easily expire under such pressure and that would have multiplied her current problems.

On learning that her father had been appointed to oversee the copper mine on the big rock her hopes were raised, for she'd always been able to manipulate him quite easily and predicted that there would be plenty of young men there to fulfil her hopes. She had every confidence that she'd get her father's agreement without any objection. As she set off on the long journey she was mulling over the prospect of obtaining a couple of strong young men to satisfy her long held desires. She revelled in the prospect of playing them off against each other.

Arriving at the copper mine in a weary state, her optimism was instantly shattered. Her father, who had never ever refused her anything, gave her an instant unequivocal rejection. Dissatisfied she followed him into the mine and repeated her request more forcefully stating that she hadn't travelled all that way for a refusal. But Flavius gave no consideration at all to his daughter's pleading.

"Enough problems of my own I've got here!" he shouted impatiently. "Production is far below requirements as it is and I've been directed to get it increased immediately. Whatever you're shouting about can't be done. I've got enough problems of my own up here," he repeated more forcefully. "Output's got to be stepped up considerably. That's why I've been sent out here. There's absolutely no one to spare

I tell you, so go back right away and stop bothering me like this! I want to hear no more about this – and that's final!"

"But surely you could spare me one!" She'd become even more determined now that her eye had landed on Geraint.

"I've told you more than once that I can spare nobody!" he ranted. "I had difficulty enough in getting you that post as it is, so you'd better make the best of it for I can't and won't help you any further!"

"Father stop being so blasted stubborn! This is vital to me! Don't you appreciate that? To succeed I desperately need better workers. Then I can show how I am able to fulfil the potential that you credit me with."

Flavius flew into a rage. "Don't you dare continue to argue with me like this! I've already told you I can spare nobody, so I want to hear no more about it! Understand?"

Geraint, hearing her appeal, wondered who could possibly argue so firmly with Flavius. He kept his sensitive ears attuned and quickly realised their relationship.

"Can't you blasted well understand, father...?" She was determined not to submit without a final attempt, but her father flew into a raging temper and smote her hard across the face.

"...Are you deaf?" he stormed. "Haven't I already

told you three times that I can do nothing for you? For the very last time I tell you I want to hear nothing more about it, so get back to those baths at Miledium immediately or I'll have the office taken from you!" Geraint noticed she'd become tense, and saw her follow her father to the rock face near him. Her chin was jutting out in anger as she continued to appeal with every step.

They stopped close to the young Celt who chanced a risky look. He was captivated by both her unconcealed rage and her attractive long flowing hair. Fortunately, Flavius had been too occupied with his daughter's behaviour to have noticed the youngster's curiosity as he witnessed the proceedings. "Just you remember who you're talking to!" he snapped, "and don't you ever dare argue with me like that again!" Flavius' sharp tone rocketed around the mine. It was followed by another resounding smack. All work momentarily stopped as he swiped his daughter hard across the face again. "I've already told you we're short of labour here as it is! All the rest of the cowardly natives seem to be hiding in the mountains, so there's very little chance of obtaining more now. The majority have become so frightened of us that they're keeping well out of our way. Do you not understand there's absolutely nothing I can do to fulfil your ridiculous demand?" He raised his voice again. "If you can't appreciate that, you must be a complete imbecile - you're no daughter of mine !

"But they're producing well here," she countered. "Can't you make this lazy lot do more, then you could spare at least one for me?" She'd set her eye firmly on Geraint. "If I don't get those baths up to standard quickly I'll be in real trouble, and that will reflect badly on you because you pleaded so forcibly for my appointment. I've already had several complaints regarding the disgraceful state of them from people who really matter. I've been told it's all got to improve and quickly and I can't possibly get anything more out of the two old men. They're all I've got! They both look as if they're ready to drop down dead on me at any moment and the authorities won't stand any further delays. My appointment was to improve the situation wasn't it? That's why you had me appointed. It was to enhance your own reputation too, wasn't it?"

He smacked her extremely hard again. "Don't you ever dare talk to me like that!"

Staggering under the blow she fell heavily against Geraint who instinctively caught her in his arm to prevent her colliding with the wall of the mine. Marcia was instantly thrilled by his semi-caress.

"Don't you dare touch her, you scum!" yelled Flavius as he hit Geraint with his fist, "and get back to your work instantly!" It was too late. The damage had already been done, for Marcia had taken a strong liking to the young Celt. Flavius turned to his daughter. "Restoring the baths is your personal problem," he stated. "You were appointed to sort it out – not me! I've done all I can for you and can do no more. It's completely up to you now. I have enough worries of my own here and can offer you nothing further." His eyes lingered again on the young Ordovice and he was puzzling even more about this sense of familiarity. It had become an obsession with him.

Marcia was completely dejected. She glared hatefully at her father for it certainly wasn't the treatment she'd expected from him. It was the very first time he'd let her down – and he'd certainly never struck her before. She realised she was starting to despise him, and she knew her hatred would become unquenchable.

Averting her eyes from her father, they lighted on Geraint's grime-covered sweaty body and she noticed the marks of her father's blows which showed prominently above his ribs. From hostility towards her father she found a certain solace in her attraction for the sinewy Celt who was exactly the type of person she'd dreamed of having. Her thrill increased as she cherished the memory of his powerful grasp. Regardless of her father she was determined to get him to the Miledium by some means or other.

Further pleading with her father would have been useless as both could be extremely stubborn. Apart from that he'd physically injured her – something he'd never ever done before and she certainly could not forgive him for that. She could be as ruthless as Flavius himself and she felt a powerful hostility towards him. After having wrestled unsuccessfully with a variety of ideas to get her own way, things suddenly changed. She was moving away despondently when she saw a soldier dash up to her father. She was fortunate to be within earshot, and she heard him inform Flavius that he was ordered to immediately take a cohort to Segontium to protect a valuable consignment of gold coming from Parys Mountain. Instantly she felt she had some hope of success and, seizing her opportunity, she dawdled until the cohort had left.

When they were out of sight she boldly approached the mine manager. "Flavius has given me permission to take one of your workers back to the Miledium," she lied knowing her father would be, by then, too far away to be consulted so she felt confident she was on quite safe ground.

"Did he say which one, then?"

"No. I'm to pick one myself."

"That's rather irregular so perhaps you'd better wait for his return."

"Surely you wouldn't want to risk infuriating him by disobeying his instructions, would you?"

"No – but…"

"…Then you're braver than me if you're prepared to be at the receiving end of his temper when he returns. I shouldn't like to face him with such news, and I'm his beloved daughter." She knew she was pushing her luck but it was her only chance; everyone was afraid of Flavius when he flew into a temper and she was determined not to let the opportunity go, regardless of any possible repercussions.

"Have you got one in mind then?"

"No," she stated deceitfully. She didn't want him to suspect anything. "I'd like to study a few closely before I finally decide." She already knew who she would choose but didn't want it to seem so obvious.

Having arranged for some half dozen to be paraded before her, among whom was Geraint, after much feigned indecision she eventually called him to her. Noticing the smug look of satisfaction on her face he decided to use it to his advantage and, appreciating who she was related to, it made it even more exciting. "You'll come with me to Miledium," she stated with an enchanting smile and he felt sure she'd thrown him a sly wink before adding, "You'll find conditions there far more acceptable than they are here, I promise you."

"But perfectly content I am here," he lied, to see how she'd respond. Although it meant the possibility of moving away from Flavius, he could see no opportunity for obtaining his revenge on him while stuck in that mine. He was also determined not to leave Alwena behind if it could possibly be avoided.

In a demonstration of her father's fury, she slapped his face hard. "Don't you dare refuse me," she howled, "and respect you'll show me too!"

Although Geraint saw her father's traits in her, he rightly sensed her nervousness and decided to use it to his advantage. "You could regret having done that one day," he hissed and her face crimsoned to confirm the lack of confidence which she'd tried to conceal. She slapped him hard again to hide her confusion.

"Don't make things difficult for yourself – or me," she added in a hushed tone not wanting anyone else to hear and he suddenly had an inspiration.

Resisting a strong desire to strike back he said, "On one condition only will I come."

"Don't you dare make demands of me!" Again, he could see the reflection of her father. Then they both noticed the North African approaching, suspecting she was having trouble. Quickly she added in an undertone, "What's your demand then?"

"This dumb one to come with me too it is," he added, nodding towards Alwena who was just passing. Very good to me he was when needed him I did. Vowed to look after him when his accident he had, I did." Seeing she was somewhat hesitant, he added, "Not to worry about his injury you are, still an excellent worker he is and no trouble at all with him you'll have, I promise you."

"The overseer came up to him and struck him with his whip. "Get back to work, you scum!" He struck him again. Geraint had already noticed that she'd reluctantly, and furtively, nodded her agreement and he inwardly sighed with relief. Whatever the conditions at Miledium, they simply had to be an improvement on the slavery of that mine and he was hoping that, from there, they'd find an easier means of escape

At that moment though, he suddenly saw a possible means of getting his own back on that overseer. He'd been working on a piece of rock which was suspended directly above the North African's head, and as the black man turned to address Marcia, Geraint wasted no time. He swiftly and savagely struck at the roof with all his strength and at the same moment grabbed Marcia and pulled her out of danger. Instantly, with an ear-splitting roar and a curtain of dust the rock came down on the overseer before he had had time to move.

Marcia was quick to react. "Hurry, bury him under the rubble!" she ordered, "and we'll have to get away as soon as we can." Assisted by Alwena who'd fortunately arrived on the scene again at that moment they quickly hid the body and, after swiftly binding their hands, Marcia led them both from the mine before the alarm was raised. "No harm will come to you," she promised, "provided you cause me no trouble. I've taken a tremendous risk over this so I won't allow anything to go wrong with it now."

As they passed the mine manager's hut he called out, "You'll never manage those despicable creatures on your own so I'd better send a couple of guards with you."

"There'll be no need for that," she said. "I'm not my father's daughter for nothing you know and I've got a sharp knife which I can use if needed." They quickly passed him and were well on their way to Miledium before there were further setbacks.

CHAPTER
XIV

Flavius continued to carry the image of Geraint all the way to Segontium. It troubled him that he couldn't recall any specific incident where he could have met the youth, yet he was convinced that he'd come across the Celt somewhere before. He mentally searched and pondered for every mile along the way, unsuccessfully wracking his brain to solve the tantalising mystery. He was determined to punish the youngster severely on his return to the mine for causing him such annoyance, whether he solved the problem or not.

His cohort had been spotted by Iorwerth who'd long been seeking signs of how to disrupt them. He'd been watching from an elevated hideout and, noticing the peculiar manner with which the leader handled his horse, he realised it was Flavius. He was certain that they were making for Segontium and he was planning to intercept them on their return.

On his way to Segontium, Flavius passed the exact spot where they'd set that successful trap for Hywel. Thoughts of that Celtic youth again entered his mind but he got no further. He couldn't resolve the matter. The longer the problem remained unsolved, the more

Flavius' temper increased. He became desperate to get back to the mine.

Iorwerth in the meantime, having been well schooled by Hywel, was taking extreme care over his preparation. He expected the cohort to be escorting gold from Parys mountain area and although he knew that the Rebels couldn't physically defeat the Romans, at least they could become an annoyance. When the Romans returned, the Rebels, from well concealed positions, bombarded them with heavy missiles hoping to cause the cohort to break ranks and enable a few of the bolder Rebels to attempt to retrieve some gold. However, that was only a remote possibility as the invaders were constantly alert and well organized.

When he tried to put the plan into practice it was miserably unsuccessful and one of Iorwerth's men was captured. Iorwerth himself had managed to escape but there was no way he could have rescued that man.

Flavius was furious. Having earmarked Iorwerth for capture, he then found himself in a similar situation to that they'd been in several times with Hywel. The dreadful Roman centurion wore a wry smile convinced he'd eventually get Iorwerth as well. "Think you can outsmart the pride of Rome, do you?" he screamed at the retreating Iorwerth. "Another leader of your horrible rabble thought that some years ago, but he hadn't bargained for meeting up with me and he met the fate he deserved." His arrogance was clear.

Flavius was incensed that they'd captured an insignificant Rebel as it meant it would delay his return to the copper mine. He'd have to take the prisoner to Deva first and make a full report. All that would delay the spiteful revenge he'd intended for Geraint, which annoyed him.

They tightly bound the captured Celt and led him to Deva with a noose about his neck for Flavius had no desire to disobey the Governor's directive this time. He'd been severely reprimanded for killing Hywel instead of returning him to Deva, and this Celt hadn't given him the embarrassment that the one who'd troubled him years before had. He considered that the Governor was welcome to make an example of the young Rebel before meting out the ultimate punishment. He could have had the satisfaction of personal involvement in the prisoner's death but was content to leave that privilege to others and allow him to go more quickly to Craig Fawr.

When the cunning Tyddyn Fach had tracked Geraint to the copper mine he'd carefully concealed himself from Roman eyes, and to redeem himself he'd hastened back to search for Mawddach. When he caught up with his chief, the tribal leader was delighted with the news. It infuriated him not to be able to capture Geraint from the copper mine but he believed that Flavius could possibly help him, if he could persuade the Roman to hand him over. Mawddach had no idea where to find Flavius but as usual Tyddyn had the answer. He'd overheard the Roman centurion being directed to Segontium and quickly informed Mawddach. The Ordovice chief knew there'd be a chance of contacting the cohort on its return provided he was prepared to wait at a suitable spot.

On the return to Deva, Flavius was surprised to come across Mawddach, and thinking he was attempting to set up an ambush, he sneered at his stupidity. The centurion had other matters on his mind and was in no mood to deal with the grovelling Ordovice chief. He had him grabbed, and when the cowardly Mawddach saw his tribesmen rounded up he blurted out the identity of Geraint. "The son of that pestilential Rebel I led you to years ago, up at the copper mine you've got," he bawled.

Flavius was annoyed that it hadn't dawned on him earlier, for it had now become so perfectly obvious. His vindictiveness increased on learning Geraint was the son of that Rebel he'd killed years before and he was amazed that he hadn't realised. He became more frustrated as he had to go to Deva with his recent captive first. He now couldn't wait to get to the mine and deal quickly with that cheeky upstart. He'd now really make him pay for all the trouble caused by his father's activities so many years previously. He was so eager to confront the youngster that he was very tempted to disregard the rules and go back to the mine but considered it was more than he dare do. The cohort immediately felt his frustration for he hurried them to Deva at breakneck speed, determined that nothing was going to prevent him from confronting the son of that former burdensome Rebel.

CHAPTER
XV

The situation at the Miledium was nothing like Geraint had expected. He'd been very disappointed to find that there was no obvious means of escape from the complex. Although he had limited freedom, wherever he went his mind was permanently dwelling on a way to escape and all his endeavours had failed. There was only one very remote chance: that was the possibility of getting over the palisade in the farthest corner in the darkness, but even that couldn't be achieved without help. In the very unlikely case of the opportunity presenting itself, it would still be impossible with Claudia continually watching him as she was. He thought she was merely being vigilant but her prime aim was to foil Marcia, who had been unable to conceal her strong attraction to the Celt.

The water for the baths was obtained from a system of aqueducts fed from outside springs and all were in such a dreadful state that they were desperately in need of cleaning. Geraint had studied them carefully and recognised there would be no chance to escape that way. Having traced them from their point of entry until they'd emerged in the baths themselves there wasn't the slightest sign of any possible escape route. The bathing area was so disgustingly dirty that he wouldn't have patronised it even had he been allowed to but he considered it good enough for the Romans whom he hated so fiercely.

As he ambled around he saw a strange new word. Frigidarium meant nothing to him, yet he studied it in puzzlement for several minutes trying to pronounce it without success. Quietly entering the changing room just inside the entrance, he discovered it was the only way out of the premises and it was always carefully guarded. There were several discarded articles of clothing lying on the floor which puzzled him. Despite using extreme stealth for his inspection of the building he'd been noticed by the attendant on duty.

"Hey, you!" he called as he rushed from the Frigidarium. What are you doing in the Tepidarium? That is no place for you unless you've been delegated to work there – and you certainly couldn't have been authorised to be there because I haven't been informed." Although slightly officious, it seemed that the attendant was pleased to have someone to talk to even if it was only a Celt.

Geraint's response was instant. "To look for a brooch she's lost the superintendent sent me," he lied. It had been so spontaneous he'd marvelled at his own reaction.

"Well it won't be here! She's not visited these

premises for days." His tone portrayed disgust that Marcia hadn't appeared to inspect the place. "I know that because she's so shifty; we continually have to keep our eyes on her to see she's not spying on us."

"Where or when she lost it she didn't tell me. Only to look for it here she sent me."

"You'd better be quick about it then, I'll not have you idling about here!" There was no doubt that he harboured suspicions that Geraint was looking for something to steal and for his own peace of mind wanted him out of the way as quickly as possible. Geraint though was determined not to leave until he'd had a thorough look to establish any possibility of escape.

Followed by the attendant, he strolled into the Frigidarium which housed the cold plunge pool. He secretly sneered at the screams of the two characters who'd jumped in and marvelled at the thought of them representing Roman strength. The giggling, screaming effeminate characters were behaving quite girlishly and he smiled as he considered what they'd have done had they faced the extremely icy waters of Llyn Llydaw on the upper reaches of Wyddfa where he'd been forced to learn to swim.

The atrium, as the only means of entry into the building, was constantly under observation from so many angles that there was no way of escaping through there. He looked hard at the cold plunge pool and was disgusted. The water looked so uninviting that he'd have been reluctant to take a dip had he been allowed to. Although he considered it to be good enough for the invading force as they deserved nothing better. He soon lost interest in the baths once he'd established there appeared to be no visible means of escape from there.

As soon as he entered the adjoining area he found the contrast remarkable. The warm dry air was quite welcome but as he wandered further he found the heavy hot atmosphere almost unbearable. He'd arrived next to the furnace, and the gabled end room was full of a dense steam which was impenetrable. He'd never experienced anything remotely like it before and quickly moved back to the Frigidarium to recheck that there was no means of escape that way. The severe drop in temperature was welcome but he involuntarily shivered before silently making his exit.

He didn't cease to be amazed at the overall disgusting state of the premises but he continually carried the layout in his mind in the hope that it might eventually serve his purpose. Dirty towels and clothing had been dropped everywhere and the whole place was desperately in need of a good clean, yet its filthy state hadn't prevented people using the pool. Although he was amused to see Romans stripped of their arrogance he was completely disgusted with the few privileged Celts who'd elected to patronize the Romans. He despised them for so shamefully associating with the invaders. As he watched, several came out of the water with bodies steaming from the intense heat then shrieked with shock as their glowing bodies hit the icy water of the plunge pool. He was very tempted to jump in after them despite the state of the water and hold their treacherous heads underneath until they could shriek no more. He was smiling as he observed their sensitivity. He remembered quite clearly how he'd had to hold his breath and bear each jolt without a murmur when he'd plunged himself into the freezing water of Llyn Llydaw. Thoughts of those early days when he'd successfully struggled to prevent Mawddach discovering his whereabouts greatly amused him. Much as he'd wanted to shout out with shock as he'd entered the paralysing water in that high lake he'd been far too fearful of attracting his uncle's attention.

As he was leaving the bathhouse he was accosted by Claudia. "What have you been doing in the bathhouse?" she demanded.

He was tempted to say he'd been looking for a means of escape but good sense prevailed.

"Wanted to see where the water from the aqueduct comes in because clean it I have to," he lied.

"Good. Well you can start cleaning it right away and I'll accept nothing short of perfection." Geraint took a dislike to the dark headed woman who was almost as privileged as Marcia herself.

They'd not been there a couple of weeks when there was a drastic change of plan. Flavius had arrived at the baths in a raging temper. Storming up to Marcia with flaming eyes he grabbed her by her tresses and slapped her face with a painfully stinging blow. "Disobeyed me about taking men from the mines, didn't you? Not one you took, but two – and killed an overseer too they did. I'm just going to the baths to remove the dust from my journey and I want them here when I come back! You're certainly going to suffer for this you know! Nothing will save you this time!" He slapped her again, more forcefully. "I'm going to the bathhouse now and if they're not here when I come back you'll certainly know about it," he warned.

Marcia's infatuation for Geraint was instantly strengthened by a newly found hatred for her father. Flavius had publicly shamed her in front of that dreadful Claudia whom she was still having difficulty controlling – and that increased her annoyance. She knew that her father's fury would spell trouble for Geraint and that made her more reluctant than ever to let him get hold of the handsome Celt that she'd become increasingly attracted to. Flavius could be a perfect beast and she knew he'd not only punish them for her disobedience but would see that they received the most excruciating torture for the death of the overseer. Immediately he got his hands on them back at the copper mine they'd truly suffer. Later, the remnants of their broken bodies, barely alive, would be taken to Deva for their final humiliation and execution. She couldn't be a party to that, especially since her father had continued to be so aggressive to her as well.

Thinking quickly, she sped through the darkness of their well-guarded compound and sent the prisoners' sentry on a futile mission. As soon as he left she urgently called Geraint and Alwena, hurriedly related the situation to them and assisted them to flee. Despite being spitefully inclined to sacrifice Geraint's friend she anticipated that he wouldn't leave alone, so to safeguard the one she was attracted to, she reluctantly felt forced to include Alwena.

Her infatuation for Hywel's son had rapidly increased since he'd been at the Miledium. Her eyes had followed his every move around the premises. She'd admired the handsome frame to such an extent that she already had the desire to find a way to spend a happy future in his company.

As she was silently leading them to that extremely dark corner of the compound which Geraint had noted on his arrival, she whispered eagerly in his ear. "I've got a small room in Deva if only you can get there. It's off the Foregate and not far from the Amphitheatre. It's just outside the walls and my father has no knowledge of it. You'll find it quite easily – there's the image of a bear on the right-hand side of the lintel and a snake on the left door jamb." Geraint was amazed that she was taking such an interest in him. "It's only a very short distance from the Amphitheatre, and if you can manage to get that far undetected, I'll definitely be able to shield you." As they reached that dark corner she wished him well.

He'd been planning fruitlessly how to break out of that complex so Marcia's assistance was like an answering prayer. She'd already protected the spikes with thick skin coverings and had provided logs for them to step on to assist them over. Geraint smiled. He considered that if only they could get safely into Deva she'd be able to inform him of her father's movements which could enable him to satisfy his revenge.

As Marcia had led them to the darkest part of the compound she was convinced that nobody had seen them. She had been unaware that Claudia, ever jealously watchful of the person who'd replaced her, had followed her stealthy movements from a distance. Seeing the two silhouettes following Marcia, her suspicions had been instantly aroused.

Marcia watched the two swiftly scale the wall and hurriedly disappear. Instantly she pulled down the skins and dismantled the heap of logs.

As she was returning to her hut Claudia stepped out of the shadows to accost her. "Whatever have you been doing out there in the shadows?" she demanded suspiciously.

"That's my business and nothing to do with you," she snapped, uncertain as to what her subordinate might have seen. "Get back to your work immediately!" she directed.

"You seem to forget that the security of these premises is as much my concern as yours," retorted her deputy. "I'm not prepared to risk lowering my status any further through anyone's reckless actions – especially yours!"

"Don't you dare be so insolent or I'll have you removed!"

"You could try – but it won't do you any good now!" Claudia had sensed that Marcia was bluffing, to get herself out of an embarrassing situation by attempting to become bold. She believed she could easily confirm her suspicions.

"Don't you dare forget that I'm in charge here and will take all responsibility for my actions without interference from you! Go and wait by the fountain and I'll come and deal with you when I'm ready."

Claudia's suspicion had been increased by Marcia's attitude and she stormed off in a pretended huff as if to obey – but she had other ideas.

Marcia sighed with relief when Claudia seemed to have left so readily without further objection. However, in her mind she was rapidly making plans for her assistant's removal. She knew full well how infuriated her father would be at her action but she was confidently prepared to face up to him. After all, she'd regularly been able to manipulate him and there was no reason for him to suspect she'd had anything to do with the young Celts' disappearance.

Instead of complying with Marcia's instruction Claudia quietly made her way to the hutment where the slaves had been housed and accosted the sentry. "Are those two young Celts still in that hut?" she enquired in as casual a tone as she could muster without arousing suspicion.

"Yes," replied the sentry, surprised at being asked, "of course!"

"Well bring them out then. I've special instructions for them."

"Come here you two," called the sentry officiously as he entered the hut. He was out within seconds in a state of concerned disbelief. "They're not there! They're nowhere to be seen!" he stated in amazement.

"Well, they're your responsibility you know so if you've allowed them to get out, you'll be severely punished." Claudia's approach was savage but inwardly she was glowing with a sense of achievement. "You've either purposely let them out or you've been negligent and deserted your post. Either is extremely serious – and you know what that means!"

"No, I'd never do such things." He was in a state

bordering on panic.

"Well you must somehow have allowed them to escape – and you'll not avoid a penalty for that!"

"No! No! I didn't!" The sentry was truly terrified. "I only left to go on an errand for the superintendent."

"I don't believe she sent you on an errand. You're using that as an excuse to cover your inefficiency."

"No really! She sent me to collect some keys that she'd left behind." He looked completely bemused. "Funny though, I couldn't find them and when I got back she wasn't here."

Claudia had received sufficient information for her purpose and knew how she'd use it. As soon as Flavius returned she excitedly related the whole incident to him and his fury surpassed even her expectations. Having confirmed what had happened from the legionnaire guarding the prisoners, Flavius instantly sought his daughter. He thrashed her with such ferocity that her clothing was left in rags; her battered face was bleeding in several places and he personally cut off the long tresses of her hair as a symbol of disgrace. "I'll no longer accept you as my daughter," he yelled. "You've put me in a very serious position by assisting those prisoners to escape. I want nothing more to do with you now or ever again! I totally disown you and will see that you get all the punishment you deserve! Even though you were my daughter you won't be spared and you've certainly not heard the last of this. You'll be returned to Deva immediately under heavy escort and dealt with in the way you deserve!"

She turned to run, but expecting such a move he caught her arm and jerked her back.

"No! No, please!" pleaded Marcia in desperation, not wanting to believe what she'd heard. That was the last thing that she'd envisaged and she certainly hadn't been prepared for it.

"Don't you dare appeal to me!" shrieked Flavius. "You've brought all this on yourself so you can expect no sympathy or mercy from me or anyone else from now on. You're completely on your own and you'll suffer the punishment we deal out to all traitors – even if I have to authorise and administer it myself."

Marcia was shaking with terror. She hadn't expected her father to treat her so vilely. She'd always known that her father was renowned for his cruelty but had never contemplated he'd ever turn that cruelty on her. She realised that if his threat was fulfilled she'd be totally disfigured for life, and screamed.

CHAPTER
XVI

Within minutes of leaving the compound an uproar emanating from the bathhouse reached the two Celts. They realised they would have to move extra fast to avoid recapture. It was fortunate that they'd made a reasonable start but they were unsure which way to go. Looking back, they saw the array of flaming torches spread in an arc over a considerable area. It seemed to be following them and getting frighteningly near. Flavius had obviously sent a sizeable number after them and the searchers seemed to be examining the ground in every direction for indications of their movements until, after a shout from one of them, they all seemed to pull away to the left.

Although the locality was completely foreign to the two it was fortunate that they'd been brought up in a similar type of terrain and they found little difficulty in making progress, despite the darkness.

"Wherever can we go?" enquired Alwena, showing much concern. Panic was evidently starting to creep into her voice and her normal reasonable composure seemed to be deserting her.

"An ancient burial ground up on a hill somewhere

around here there is, I once heard say. On rocky ground too it is, so up there a cave of some kind there could be. Hide there perhaps we could if lucky we are."

"Trusting to luck is no good. Sure, we've got to be!"

"Better than stopping around here and arguing like this, it is," he responded sharply.

"Gaining ground on us the Romans might be by now. We've simply got to make for somewhere!" He grabbed her hand and pulled her roughly along. They were heading up hill in a south easterly direction and it was a struggle all the way. Fortunately, the Romans weren't following. Having to contend with such wild terrain they were not certain that they were heading in the right direction, but luck was with them. The night was particularly dark but their eyes had now become accustomed to it so that they could identify the burial ground when they eventually stumbled upon it.

The Romans, having expected them to have covered as much distance as they could, had assumed that they wouldn't have attempted to escape up such a steep hill, as that route would have greatly reduced their speed. So, anticipating they'd have kept to the lower ground, they concentrated their search down there.

To Geraint's delight, shortly after reaching the burial ground he found a small cave in a nearby rocky outcrop. On entering he accidentally kicked the skull of a dead sheep. The noise he'd created was followed by an almost inaudible whimper and a hasty movement. They both stood still with shock as a twelve-year-old lad rushed at them with a knife. Having been disturbed from his sleep by their entry his action had been amazingly swift. Fortunately, Geraint had noticed the glint of the metal in time and as the youngster dashed towards him in his attempt to get out of the cave he grabbed his stringy little wrist very firmly, and received a slight slash for his effort.

"Ow, let me go!" screamed the youngster as he unsuccessfully tried to bite Geraint who'd been twisting his arm to make him drop the knife. Geraint gave him a severe smack across the face. "Ow!" bawled the lad again as he struggled harder to free himself.

"Who are you and what are you doing up here?" demanded Geraint.

"Ask you the same I can," replied the lad insolently. "Not one of us, from the way you speak you are, and thankfully not a blasted Roman either!" He seemed to concentrate for a few seconds. "One of those hated Ordovice you must be then!"

Geraint grabbed him by his jerkin and raised him to eye level. The youngster didn't flinch; he returned Geraint's stare unwaveringly in the darkened cave.

"No concern of yours who we are," stated the older one firmly as he kicked the knife out of the cave entrance. "All Celts we are and together we must work to rid our land of these Roman invaders."

"Not trust you, I do. Saying that to save me calling for help you are! Who are you and why come here have you anyway?"

Geraint was now seeing the sinewy lad more clearly, and noticed he had a certain resolve about him. The darkened teeth were fixed in a snarl and the Ordovice was forced to admire the lad's courage for standing up to him as he did. "Who are you?" Geraint demanded roughly as he shook the somewhat frail, but determined, body to knock the spirit out of him. "And what are you doing holed up here on your own like this?"

"Arwyn, I am," he responded just a little more shakily than before as if his confidence had weakened. Deceangli, and proud of it, I am too. To this terrible part of the land we were brought by the Romans and run away to try to get help I did. Tad and three brothers in that awful lead mine I left. Kill them the way those Roman beasts make them work they will. Tried to make me work too, but escaped I did see, and not let them get me again, I will!" Geraint admired the determination in his voice. "Kill myself before that, I will!" He surprisingly showed not a trace of panic. "You're not going to give me over to them, are you?"

Geraint smiled. "No, we'll not give you up, but what to do with you I don't know. You just can't stay here for ever you know."

"All right up here I am. Know the land well I do

– even if it is rugged land," he added in a tone of contempt. "Know how to look after myself too I do."

Geraint had little doubt about his ability in that respect from what he'd seen of him. "How will you manage then?" he enquired with interest.

"Plenty of hiding places up here like this I've got." He seemed completely capable of taking care of himself and that really impressed Geraint.

"But it's not safe for you to hide up here like this with all these Romans about."

"Not bother to come up here they will, so think nothing about it I do. Only rocks there are up here and expecting to get ambushed they are if they do come, so they stay away." His reasoning seemed quite sound for one so young. It made him appear much older than his years.

"Good. Until tomorrow then, up here we'll stay. Then when it gets dark, with less chance of being caught, we'll leave."

"Who from you running, then?"

"Romans of course."

The boy still seemed uncertain of Geraint.

"No trouble if you in the dark travel, but where will you go?"

"To the Roman fortress at Caer – Deva as the Romans call it – if we're not caught."

Arwyn flinched. He suspected Geraint had been sneakily snooping for the Romans. His eyes strayed outside the cave searching for the knife but Geraint had kicked it well out of reach.

"Friends of those horrible Romans then you must be after all, if to Caer you're going!" There was no concealing the boy's concern. He'd suddenly become worried.

"No. To see if there's any way to get our tribesmen inside that fortress to create trouble we're going." It all sounded feeble enough but it prevented him giving details.

"Not believe you, I do," stated the boy in panic. He snatched his wrist away and was instantly through a very small hole in the back of the cave. Although Geraint tried to follow, the child had been extremely quick. The opening was too small to allow him through, but it had completely swallowed Arwyn.

Geraint and Alwena concealed themselves in the cave all the following day. They believed they had not been seen, but Arwyn had been waiting for them to emerge. Having exited the cave along that secret route he'd busied himself looking for the knife without which he felt completely naked. He'd had ideas of turning the tables on the two whom he believed to be Roman sympathisers. As a Deceangli himself, he'd been brought up to detest and distrust the other tribe and he didn't feel satisfied until he found the knife he'd been looking for.

CHAPTER
XVII

As darkness closed in the following night, Geraint suggested they move. Stealthily leaving the cave, they started on their way but the young boy, doubtful of their motives, had been watching them closely and followed them at a distance hoping in some way to upset their plans should they attempt to liaise with the Romans.

Alwena pointed out the numerous flaming torches which were still glowing far down to the left and they realised that Flavius was continuing the search for them. To avoid those Romans, they had stumbled blindly into what they later considered was a Roman stronghold. As they'd been hastening along what they had considered would be a safe route, they were suddenly surprised by a Roman soldier approaching from the left. They'd exercised extreme caution so they noticed him soon enough, but he'd been intensely alert. Fortunately he was still some way off when he suddenly challenged.

"Hey, you! Stop!" he yelled. The two young Ordovices took to their heels on the first syllable of his command. As they went they heard him bellow to his colleagues. "Hey there! I've found them! Hurry!

They've just passed this spot and ran off when I challenged them."

In their panic, Geraint and Alwena abandoned all attempts at caution to run away as fast as they could. With no trappings to hinder them they had an excellent start on the more heavily clad Romans, even though those foreigners were at the peak of their fitness. They made good headway by twisting and changing course until they were desperately short of breath. Gasping with pain they plunged deep into a wood to conceal themselves. Once safe within the dense thicket they managed, with difficulty, to scale a tree which enabled them to remain perfectly well hidden within its stout leafy branches, while the Romans pounded the ground immediately below them.

Unbeknown to them, Arwyn, who'd also been following, had scaled another tree not far away wondering what they would do.

They stayed, protected by the autumnal tinted leaves, for a considerable time. Even when they considered it safe enough to move, they still delayed their descent to ensure they wouldn't be falling into a trap. As they were finally descending Alwena unfortunately lost her footing and fell heavily to the ground, twisting her ankle severely. With great presence of mind, and with a massive intake of breath, she stifled her cry in case the Romans were still within range. Instead, emitting a subdued curse, she grabbed her excruciatingly painful right ankle knowing that she'd now become a very serious liability. When Geraint moved off she bravely limped after him.

"By yourself now you'll have to go Geraint," she said as the pain became more intense. It had severely hindered her progress. "With a foot like this no use to you I'll be."

"Nonsense you talk Alwena. In this together we are. Not desert you now that this far we've come I will."

"But hardly move I can, really! The pain is dreadful when on my foot I put my weight. You really must leave me. If stay here for long we do, we'll be caught."

"I'll never leave you on your own you know. There'll be more chance of them catching you then and I'd hate to think of the consequences if that happened. Nothing has changed, you know, as far as we're concerned. Yes, I agree, we certainly must leave. We'll have to go through the night and find somewhere to shelter during the day. If we keep to the high ground as far as we can we'll probably be able to see what turns up."

They moved stealthily along the high ground and were relieved to note they didn't appear to be followed by Romans any longer although, unbeknown to them, young Arwyn was still only a short distance behind. They assumed that the search was bound to resume at first light so to avoid being silhouetted against the sky, visible to any wandering Roman, if the moon broke through they used as much cover as possible. Progress was tremendously slow due to Alwena's situation and, having travelled as far as they could before dawn, the ordeal had completely drained her.

As daylight crept in they sought shelter in an overgrown thicket hoping to be missed by any pursuing Roman. They could still hear the searchers scouring the area in the distance but were fortunate that the hunt came nowhere near them.

Geraint cautiously emerged as dusk fell and through the trees caught sight of a large group of buildings. Although it was some distance below them, there was an element of hope if only they could reach it unobserved. "Take a chance and make for it we'll have to," he announced pointing it out to her.

Alwena's painful ankle was still causing her immense trouble. "Not that far with a foot like this can I go Geraint," she complained.

"Try you'll have to, won't you?" he stated with as firm a kindness as he could raise. We simply can't stay out here again all night. It already feels colder and last night was bad enough wasn't it? All right you'll be if help you I do, and very slowly we go, isn't it?" It took them quite some time to struggle down to the buildings which consisted of several timber constructions set out in a rectangular fashion.

Arwyn was puzzled as he continued to stalk them

and wondered with increasing suspicion what they were up to.

Although Alwena was suffering acute pain she gritted her teeth and bore things courageously. They heard no sound as they approached the first building, apart from the snort of a horse stabled near the extremity of a small block, and their hopes rose. "Looks as if this could do us nicely," whispered Geraint having taken a closer inspection. He'd found an empty animal shelter at the very end of the block. "Dry and comfortable for the night it will be and allow time for your ankle to improve too."

Arwyn, who'd witnessed them go in, squeezed himself into a small gap on the opposite side of the compound to await developments. Now he was more convinced than ever that they were some sort of Roman collaborators.

A little later Geraint heard voices approaching and strained his ears to know what was being said.

"I'd better see if that horse is all right after its fall." The statement, delivered with a note of reluctance, carried clearly on the still night air and was equally distinct to Arwyn who was becoming completely baffled by the developments. "I don't want that damned Sebastian on my back again!" complained the speaker. "He's a perfect pest these days!" He paused momentarily. "I suppose I'd better check that empty shelter at the end too – or he'll want to know why I didn't."

Geraint was grateful for the warning but experienced a touch of panic. He realised that if they were found, there was no way Alwena could get away quickly enough in her crippled state. He hurriedly helped her into a hay rack protruding from the wall at the back. There was a friendly whinny from the horse next door as if it was responding to the voice of the man talking to it.

"You're going next door in a couple of days old boy so don't make such a fuss. I'll go and make sure it's ready for you in a minute."

Geraint had successfully managed to get Alwena into the hay rack and covered her with hay when he heard the door of the adjoining shelter close and the unmistakable sound of the man's footsteps coming closer. He knew he had to move fast for there was no way he could conceal himself as well in the time. "Perfectly still keep and don't move," he instructed in an urgent whisper. "Tomorrow night I'll come back for you. A better chance of getting away in the dark then we'll have."

At that moment, the door opened and the solitary legionnaire holding a smoking torch stood amazed as he stared at Geraint. Without giving the Roman time to think, Hywel's son charged straight at him and butted him viciously in the stomach. The torch flew backwards into the yard and lay burning on the ground but Geraint had fled into the night and when the other legionnaire came dashing to see what had happened Geraint was nowhere in sight.

"What cheek!" gasped the winded victim. "A blasted saucy young Celt was hiding in there! Probably trying to steal a horse, I suppose."

"Well it'll be a complete waste of time trying to chase him now in this darkness," his colleague stated. "These thieving natives are becoming a load of proper trouble makers these days and he could be anywhere by now. Still if we mount a full-scale search as soon as it's light we're bound to find him."

It was exactly what Geraint had hoped for. He'd made as much distance from the place as he could, trusting to luck that Alwena wouldn't be discovered.

Arwyn, witnessing the incident from his shelter, wondered what had happened to Alwena. He'd started to change his mind about them both and now considered Geraint with an element of admiration. It had now been made perfectly obvious to him that the Ordovicians were not in league with the Romans but it puzzled him to think that Alwena had been abandoned. He hurriedly followed Geraint again to find out more.

Towards nightfall the following day Geraint slowly and carefully made his way back to the site. There was a legionnaire positioned at the door of the shelter making it impossible for him to attempt to enter that way. Worried for Alwena's safety, he wondered if she'd been found and what they would have done with her. After cautiously making his way to the back of the building he carefully scratched the wood behind her stall in a similar manner to that in which they had communicated with each other in their earlier days. There was no reply and his heart missed a beat. He was unsure whether they'd taken her. He tried again, a little louder hoping it wouldn't be heard by the guard, and was relieved to receive a gentle response. It was so very faint that he'd almost missed it.

The legionnaire on duty was joined by a friend. "It seems you're enjoying a stint as nursemaid to an empty stable again," he mocked.

"Sebastian's a proper pig making me stand here all night like this. He should know that the stupid young Celt won't have the nerve to come back. Surely even he's got more sense than to attempt that. Sebastian seems to have lost his head over this - sticking me out here. He must think that there's nothing better for me to do."

"There's no knowing what that youngster was up to though. Some are stupid enough to try anything."

Geraint had already got his fingers behind a wood panel and was attempting to ease it out gently, but it refused to move. He was forced to exert more pressure and the wood suddenly gave way with a resounding crack. The young Celt held his breath and retreated quickly.

"What was that?" enquired the guard.

"That stupid old horse next door, I suppose," offered his friend. "He's everlasting kicking the blasted woodwork, trying to get out. That was how he damaged his leg in the first place. I'll just go and see what damage he's done this time."

Before he got back Geraint had managed to get Alwena out and, with Geraint's help, she was hobbling away into the night as quickly as she could.

Noticing their difficulty, Arwen realised it wouldn't be long before the Romans came to realise what had happened and gave chase. To lay a false trail, he quickly grabbed a large armful of hay from the hole in the back of the stall and hurriedly discarded small strands of it in the opposite direction to which the Ordovices had gone to assist them in their escape.

"Safer going south we will be," Geraint told Alwena. "Less risk of meeting Romans that way it will be," He hoped he sounded far more convincing than he felt.

When the two legionnaires entered the shelter with flaming torches and saw the hay scattered from the rack and the gaping hole behind it, the guards were dumbfounded.

"That certainly wasn't there when I looked in yesterday," one said, hardly believing his own eyes, "and nobody has reported it either." Following a cursory examination at the back a little later, they came across the distinct trail of hay and wasted much time in swiftly following it. However, Arwyn had been far too wily to be caught and having discharged all the hay to a fair distance he'd swung round in pursuit of the other Celts.

CHAPTER
XVIII

They forced themselves to travel through the night. Despite Alwena's affliction they were amazed at the distance they'd travelled. They'd stuck valiantly to the high ground once more, believing it would be their safest route despite Alwena still being in extreme pain. The initial commotion behind them had been horrendous and had spurred them on to even greater efforts. They were amazed and relieved when they realised that the noise was diminishing, for the chasing group seemed to be moving in the opposite direction.

At the break of day, they came across another cave and, believing they were not being followed, holed up there for a very welcome rest. Unbeknown to them, the sneaky Tyddyn Fach had spotted and followed them, but Mawddach's lackey had been unaware that he too was being watched. Arwyn had been puzzled by the thin Ordovice's suspicious actions and rightly concluded he was up to no good. Both Geraint and Alwena, feeling the strain after their efforts, entered the cave, quickly found a reasonably comfortable spot and instantly dozed off. They slept well, Geraint waking when the sun was high in the sky. Going to the entrance he cautiously surveyed the scene and rubbed his eyes in disbelief. A few fields away he saw the unmistakable figure of Peris. There was no doubt about the identity for his attire clearly identified him and that peculiar, unique stagger assured him that it was the druid he knew.

"Inside there, stay," he commanded Alwena. "I've just seen Peris and I want to catch up with him."

"Sure it was him, are you? I don't want you falling into a trap and leaving me alone."

"I'll not leave you. I'll soon be back," he promised. "I can hardly believe he's travelled this far without a good reason. It must be something really serious."

"You must be very careful then," she warned. "I tell you it could be a trap; someone might be following him."

"No trap it is. There's no doubt that it's Peris. I'd know his walk anywhere. He's so careful about being seen by the Romans now that he doesn't take chances."

Geraint hurried after the religious man and the priest was surprised to see him.

"Whatever out here are you doing?" enquired the druid.

"The same about you I can say," replied Geraint. He then told his story in detail. The vestured man was extremely concerned and quickly assessed the danger they were in especially with Alwena in such a crippled condition. He expressed his worry for them.

"Surprised to see you out here anyway, I am," stated Geraint hoping the druid would tell him the reason for being so far from his native environment.

"Surveying the land, I am to see if any help to Iorwerth I can be."

"Iorwerth?"

"Yes. Taken by the Romans he's been and held captive in Deva I believe he is now. How to reach him I don't know. What they'll do with him will not be pleasant. Concerned I am about what will happen to him and not much time we've got, I think!"

Geraint was severely taken aback. He didn't want to believe the dreadful news.

Knowing Iorwerth had always been so careful he wondered if he'd also been betrayed.

"Sure, you are Druid?"

"Oh yes, taken three days ago, he was. Not far from where your poor father was murdered. That same vile Roman it was too!"

Geraint was horrified, knowing Iorwerth would receive no mercy at the hands of Flavius. "Try to get to him then I will," he stated in impulsive desperation. "I must really find a way to get into that Deva stronghold. We just can't leave Iorwerth in that brute's hands: so much to Tad and me he's meant. Simply got to do something to help him I have. Iorwerth thinks I'm no good, believes I've let him down – and a very big score to settle with that wicked centurion I have too."

"But you can't leave Alwena in such a crippled state. More help than ever now she'll want. There'll be a much bigger risk of her being caught if left on her own she is!" Geraint was plunged into a quandary. He fully appreciated the druid's argument but was also determined to try to help Iorwerth. "A shack not too far from here there is. You could hide there until fit enough again Alwena is. To Ceinwen it belongs and a very good healer she is too. She'll know how best to look after Alwena." He paused in thought. "Where is Alwena now, then?"

"In a cave, higher up there." Geraint pointed in the general direction.

"Come up with you then, I will. I'll take you both to Ceinwen. She'll soon get her right again."

Geraint gratefully accepted the offer and they all moved off very slowly with Alwena supported by the two males. But none of them realised they were being followed. Tyddyn, having noted the young Celts' entrance into the cave, had also spotted Peris, so mischievously decided to follow him also, to keep full knowledge of whatever was happening. He wasn't at all sure what to expect, but when he saw Geraint approach the druid he became wildly excited. He followed them to the entrance of the cave without being seen, saw them collect Alwena and struggle with the crippled girl as speedily as they could. He continued to discreetly tag on behind to see where they were going. He was so intent on his mission that he was unaware that he too was being followed. Arwyn's suspicions of Tyddyn had increased when he realised that the thin Ordovice had been so intent on secretly following his two fellow tribes-people and he was extremely puzzled over the possible motive.

Despite the assistance of the other two, Alwena was still in severe pain. Having serious trouble in moving, she stoically bit her lip to endure the agony until they eventually arrived at Ceinwen's shack. Two ponies were lightly tethered outside and a handful of chickens were scratching the ground surrounding the extremely humble dwelling. As soon as Alwena found she could relax it was an immense relief.

When Tyddyn noticed the druid leave he made no attempt to follow him. The priest had been sufficiently useful in leading him to the youngsters whom Mawddach so badly wanted, and, deciding there might be something more interesting in Ceinwen's place, he decided to prolong his stay to see what other information he could glean before reporting back to his chief.

After examining Alwena's leg, Ceinwen instantly applied a freezing cold rag to her ankle and induced her to rest. The initial shock was severe but she propped it up on a nearby log and was relieved to experience that the pain was starting to ease somewhat. "Better it will be in no time if move you don't," suggested Ceinwen as she fussed over the girl in a motherly fashion. She turned out to be quite a knowledgeable person. She stated that she didn't know Iorwerth personally, but was devastated to learn that a fellow countryman had been taken all the way to Deva for she believed the situation sounded drastic. "Bad that is," she stated. "To get him out of there not much chance there will be. Full of Romans and no time for us they have."

"But get him out I've got to," swore Geraint frenziedly. "Most trusted friend of my tad he was, so somehow I've got to get into Deva! I owe it to him!" His desperation was evident.

"Not easy that will be. On all gates are guards they say. Watch people going in and coming out they do. Not easy at all it is," she repeated.

"To help is there anybody?"

Ceinwen was thinking hard. "Well, Twm the Hayman might help you."

"Where lives Twm the Hayman and how can I get there?"

"On the banks of the Afon Dyfrydwy his home is. A long way from here that is. A field at a place called Holtinium he looks after. Tell you how to get there I will, but a long way it is," she repeated. She explained in detail the safest possible route and added, "Although it will be longer, better to keep to the high ground going south as far as the Esclusham Mountains. From there in an easterly direction go and eventually you'll get to Holtinium. Well known to everyone there Twm is. Soon find him you will."

"Not without me you'll go," screamed Alwena and although it would be difficult for her he knew she was right. They'd come so far together it would have been most unfair to abandon her now. Apart from that she would probably be useful, for she'd often sensed danger before him.

"Not really fit enough you are see," he said disappointedly looking down on her raised leg.

"Two days give me then and all right I'll be." He knew that she'd persevere even if she wasn't ready.

CHAPTER
XIX

Two days later Geraint was anxious to get started. Having thanked Ceinwen they set off planning to keep well away from the direct route to Deva. They travelled south towards the Esclusham Mountains. They'd been advised that, when they reached there, they should turn in a more easterly direction to achieve their objective. They could not risk being intercepted before they got to Twm the Hayman so they concentrated on avoiding being seen. They were still unaware that Tyddyn was following. Before they'd gone half a dozen miles they were hailed by a high-pitched, friendly voice. Turning with trepidation they found it was Arwyn who was dashing after them on one of Ceinwen's ponies. His straggly hair billowed behind him as he rode bareback so expertly. "Alwena can ride this little beast and not struggling with that leg then she will be." His sympathy for Alwena's agony had caused him to unobtrusively help himself to the pony. Geraint was puzzled. He wondered how the youngster had come across Ceinwen and why she hadn't provided the animal earlier. Nevertheless, he was so grateful he didn't ask how or why the young boy came to be following them.

"Coming after you for a long time, a thin man has been." He pointed back in the direction where Tyddyn was hiding. The snoopy little Ordovice, realising he'd been exposed, hurriedly disappeared again. Having gleaned sufficient information to carry to Mawddach he considered he now had every chance of redeeming himself so believed there was no further need to linger and quickly made off.

Geraint led Alwena at an extremely slow pace and they had several minor setbacks. On two occasions, different groups of prowling Romans very nearly intercepted them. Regardless, they eventually arrived within reach of their destination. Although the journey had been arduous, arriving at Holtinium they had no difficulty in finding Twm.

Immediately he told them they'd been extremely lucky not to have been caught, as a group of Romans had visited him the day before. They'd been searching for two young escapees and it was only because he was so useful in supplying hay to the Deva Garrison that he hadn't had his shack torched. Instead, they'd covered every corner of his dwelling in their search before departing.

"Aggressive lot, like, they were too. Some hay in Deva now, they said they wanted. Very carefully checked my permit they did and if I don't get some hay there quickly they'll be back. That was an obvious threat!"

That statement gave Geraint hope. "How do you get to Deva then?" he enquired with interest.

"Impossible for most people it is, but a special pass I have. Any time with hay I can get in. A lot of insults from the guards I must take but I put up with that if denarii I get out of it. Not always get paid I do, though."

"Concerned about Iorwerth I am," Geraint confided. "Holding him prisoner they are and somehow I must try to rescue him. I'm worried that I'll be too late already."

"Not too late yet you'll be. Nothing 'til the middle of November they'll do to him."

"Are you sure? How do you know that?"

"This time of the year all prisoners are kept until the big feast."

"What big feast?"

"Celebrate four important gods on that day they do."

"What gods they are?"

"Ceres, Juno, Minerva and Jupiter. Make of it a big day they do. Rest day for the oxen and ox drivers too it is."

"When will that be then?"

"The day after when the moon is full."

"Two weeks from now that is then. Still time to attempt something, there is. Worth trying it will be.

With your pass I could take hay tomorrow," he said hopefully.

Twm looked startled. "Oh, dangerous for me that would be if caught you were."

"We'll not get caught," stated Geraint with a note of confidence. "We've had a lot of practice dodging the Romans or we wouldn't be here now."

"Journey will not be easy and a tremendous risk for me it will be, but proper determined you seem."

"Determined I am," he confirmed, "and if not prepared to help a fellow Celt you are, then some other way I'll have to find." Geraint was trying to put pressure on him.

Twm gave the matter much thought. "If that determined you are, then help you I will."

"Good but how do I get there?"

"To the river, I go. Sometimes cross over by the first ford, I do. Just shallow enough when the river is high as it is now although still difficult in places with stones and the like it is. Keep alongside all the way from there until just outside Deva I get and, although hard going it always is, after this wet weather much harder it will be. Floods more easily on the other side though it does. Churned up ground there will be after this rain. A longer walk to Deva that way, but usually safer, it is. When not possible that way, on this side I go until near Deva and cross the ford then by that weir. Once into Deva, straight to the mansio near the stables I go. More direct that is mind, but the ford there is uneven and difficult. To get across with that old cart when the river is high, like now, is harder. Still manage though you should if very careful you are. Guards both ways there are and although I've got a pass to get inside Deva, not kind to me they are. Once at the mansio, I rest for the night in a corner of the stable before I return. Supposed not to though, but the long walk in one direction pushing that heavy cart is enough. Only when they've come a long way on horses are they allowed to use it. Coming back the same day would be real agony though; that's why I risk staying. Lots of places to hide there if you look round carefully and nobody has found me yet, for which I'm thankful. For Romans only those places are supposed to be, when they've come such a long way on horses. Lucky not to have been seen yet I am." He smiled as he remembered his guile. "Across the ford by the weir you'll find the outside guard post. More trouble still when you go that way. Dreadfully insult me those guards do; make me very cross but smile to myself I do when I take their dirty lucre. Most at the guard posts know me. They laugh at my poor old cart and mock me too."

"What chances of passing them do you think I've got?"

"Small the chances are. Not into the fortress proper I'm allowed to go. Only to the mansio."

"Could I get away with taking it instead of you?"

"A significant risk for me that would be, isn't it? Bound to ask questions they are. Know me, so don't worry they do when I get there. Difficult though for you they might make it."

"We'll not get through without taking some sort of a risk." He was amazed at his own confidence.

"By yourself you must go. Not two of you through they will let."

"But to find Iorwerth, Alwena I'll need for help!"

"Real trouble then I'll be in if caught you are. Kill me then they would."

"Tell them I attacked you on your way and stole your cart, I would."

Twm was obviously not happy with the suggestion and became very sombre.

"Not believe that they will! Always think I'm trying to trick them, they do!"

Geraint became desperate. He explained passionately that it was their only possible chance and implored him frantically for his co-operation.

After pondering for some time Twm eventually agreed but with great reluctance.

CHAPTER
XX

As they were both preparing to leave, Arwyn had deceitfully disobeyed Geraint's instruction. He didn't return the animal to Ceinwen as he'd been instructed but was still following them on it. He was eager to keep up with them and not be discovered but the beast had its own ideas and, when it got too close for Arwyn's liking, as he tried to turn it sharply away the pony let out a loud snort. Geraint's reaction was swift. Grabbing the long unruly hair of the boy he yanked him off the animal and Alwena managed to secure the pony.

"Hello," said the youngster cheekily as if he'd been generously invited.

"Whatever are you doing here now again? Told you to return that pony to Ceinwen didn't I? Following us again though you are, isn't it?"

"'Course," admitted the youngster even more cheekily.

"What are you after then, you little horror?" He gave the lad's hair a sharp tweak.

"Ow! Let me go!" yelled the boy.

"Why are you following us?" questioned Geraint, twisting his hair once more to make him face him.

"Know where you're going I do, and coming with you I am. To get into that fortress my help you'll need," stated the youngster smugly.

"Not be able to help us get in there you will!"

"Four times I've been in, see – and got out again!"

Geraint didn't believe him. He thought it was merely some childish boastful fantasy. He became angry. "How do you know we're going to Deva, anyway?"

"Heard you tell Twm, I did."

Geraint was amazed to learn that he'd been anywhere near when they'd met Twm.

"You're certainly not coming – and just take that horse back to Ceinwen like I told you!"

"You won't manage on your own – and help Alwena needs, doesn't she, for she can hardly walk!"

"We'll manage all right and you'd better get Ceinwen's pony back before she worries that the Romans have taken it."

Arwyn was deflated. He'd aimed to share the excitement of entering Deva again and was looking forward to the risks it would entail. He'd have been delighted to show off his prowess to them both by evading the Romans in their own stronghold and was disappointed when he realised that the Ordovice would never give way.

Fortunately, Arwyn had been so impressed with Ceinwen he didn't want to upset her. Reluctantly, for that reason, he decided to return the animal. He'd not considered that Ceinwen might have endangered herself by searching for a supposedly stolen pony so he felt there was no point in arguing further. He set off at a rush determined to catch up with Geraint again at the earliest possible moment. In his haste, he'd failed to take sufficient care and was shocked when Tyddyn stepped into his path causing the pony to swerve and throw him off.

"Take you to Mawddach Du I will now, and tell him where those two are going you will. All about them you will tell him too!"

"Not to that horrible Ordovice will I go. Neither you, nor anyone else will make me see!" stated the boy as he struggled unsuccessfully to wriggle out of Tyddyn's grasp.

Mawddach's hound had been recovering slowly from its wounds several miles away but as soon as it was reasonably improved it seemed to be intent on picking up Geraint's trail again. In its desperation, it sniffed all around until successful and, having found what it had been searching for, bounded off at as great a speed as it could muster. It soon exhausted itself and after an enforced pause it finally caught up with Arwyn at the very moment he'd been accosted by Tyddyn. Though still reasonably fatigued, its detestation of the sneaky Ordovice was so great that it raised sufficient energy to threaten him. The coward was so terrified that he released the child and made off before the weakened animal gave chase.

Arwyn was so grateful for its intervention that he sympathetically patted the hound and spent some time encouraging it to rise again. Although the animal feebly licked his hand in gratitude it remained panting and gasping for breath.

The young Celt was in a dilemma. He was unsure whether to return the pony, pursue Geraint, or spend time tending to the hound. He thought of Ceinwen's concern for the pony and when he saw the animal eating grass some distance away his mind was made up. He couldn't risk such a friendly creature falling into Roman hands but believed that if he hurriedly returned the pony he could still follow Geraint and Alwena, for he still judged they'd need his help in their endeavour to sneak into Deva.

O bviously due to her injury Alwena's help was limited. Regardless, as they set off she assisted as well as she could and they pushed that heavy load along the route described by Twm. The going was reasonable at first but when they came to the shallow ford they halted to study the situation in detail.

"Cross here, we can't," stated Alwena positively.

"Why can't we?" questioned Geraint. "Easy enough it looks."

"All those stones, see. Cross there without trouble with this cart we'll not!"

"No trouble that will be." Geraint had already made up his mind, for Twm had said it would be much less of a problem to get into Deva from the far side of the river.

"Well, no more help from me you'll get if that way you try to go – and not by yourself you'll manage it."

"Alwena, come on," he coaxed. "Once over there, a shorter distance it is and no more problems we'll have."

"A hard one to cross it is," she insisted. "Difficult on the other side too it will be. Flooded over there it is, can't you see?"

"Only for a little way that will be, isn't it?"

"Much more water further on there could be which we can't see from here. Wet through already I am and not more soaked I'm going to be!"

"We've not come all this far to stop now. Come on, we've got to try to help Iorwerth haven't we?"

"Better help we'll give him if to this side, we keep."

As they were arguing a burly man dashed up to them and accosted them. "Thinking of crossing this ford with that load you seem to be," he challenged in a tone which suggested he'd prevent any attempt they made.

"Considering it we were," offered the Ordovice chief's estranged nephew, his confidence waning.

"Not cross it you will until pay me you do." He greedily held out his hand which resembled a large slab of meat.

Geraint was confused: Twm had said nothing about having to pay.

"Pay you? Why? Nothing about pay Twm said."

"Strangers around here you are then? To pay me that old man didn't tell you? Never to me would he give any money, and to those damned Romans going you are by the look of you!"

"Yes, taking hay for Twm the Hayman we are."

The man became more aggressive. "Oh, that old twister's cart, then is it? Pandering to these horrible invaders always he is. Twice now you'll pay me! Dodges me every time he crosses this ford he does, so out of you I'll get it now! Always taking hay to those murdering Romans, so he must get some money from them. Using you to try to save paying me now is he?" The river dweller spat out his venom.

"To try to free one of our people held captive in Deva we're going."

"Lies! Impossible that is. Inside there you'll never get, even if cross this ford I let you – and still pay me you will or no further you will go!" The powerful-looking man was turning nasty and Geraint could see no way of appeasing him. He most certainly couldn't pay him for he'd never ever had any money, but the brute was standing firm; he seemed completely resolved not to let them pass. Just then the man received an urgent call.

"Tad! Tad!" The approaching man was instantly recognised as his son. "Coming some Romans are! Not so far off too they are, see!"

The aggressor made no further demands but instead disappeared rapidly into the undergrowth with his son. They seemed to have had a very well prepared bolt hole for both were out of sight within seconds and the two Ordovices were left to face the oncoming Romans alone.

"Quick, into those bushes as fast as you can go!"

urged Geraint. "Not too far though. Lie down where you can't be seen but you mustn't move!" He indicated a concealed spot opposite where the other two had gone, knowing that she had sufficient skills to avoid detection for he didn't want her held to ransom.

Despite the obvious pain in her ankle, Alwena hurriedly managed to conceal herself beneath a pile of fallen leaves before the soldiers arrived. She couldn't see what was happening but could clearly hear them speak.

"What have we got here?" demanded the leader hopefully. Geraint recognised him as the cruel Lucius, second in command to that hated Flavius and knew he could be as beastly as the centurion himself. "Who are you and what are you doing here?" he questioned roughly. Although anxious, Geraint was grateful that it wasn't the centurion himself.

"Taking hay to Deva, I am," he explained with no intention of saying who he was.

"Twm the Hayman's the only one allowed into Deva with hay, declared the soldier.

"Taken ill, he is and your people have demanded a load of hay to get there as quickly as possible, so he asked me to take it for him straight away."

Tyddyn the Ordovice sneak had resumed his stealthy pursuit at a distance. Once more, well within range, he'd witnessed Alwena concealing herself. It would have been so easy for him to inform on her and although tempted to, he deliberately refrained. He anticipated he'd receive a far greater personal benefit if he redeemed himself with Mawddach when he knew where Geraint was. His chief would then certainly inform Flavius, and Mawddach would have made sure that both Geraint and Alwena had been caught. He wanted to play it safe for he knew how evasive she could be and he didn't want her escaping in case she could summon help from somewhere.

Although the Roman spokesman seemed hesitant about letting Geraint go, he was obviously weighing up which would be the more advantageous – to prevent Deva receiving much needed hay or enrolling another much wanted, though probably unwilling, muscular Celt for the dreadful lead mines. He certainly wasn't going to allow his legionnaires the indignity of hauling that terribly heavy-looking Celtic hay cart all the way to Deva. After much thought, he let Geraint pass, raising a cruel laugh as the powerful young Ordovice struggled desperately to get the cart moving again. "If you can't do better than that, those damned horses will be dead before you get that stuff to Deva to feed them." He was still chuckling as he moved his group off.

CHAPTER
XXII

A lwena waited patiently for some time before she moved. She had to make certain that the Romans had gone. When she did finally move, it was with immense difficulty. She'd been so cramped up in that confined space that she'd become painfully stiff. Afraid of drawing attention to herself, she'd prolonged and endured that cooped up posture in agony. At the first attempt to get to her feet her legs had buckled. She'd panicked slightly, wondering whether she'd really be able to accompany Geraint after all. She had no doubt that he'd have found a decent hiding place and would be waiting for her.

Tyddyn was also confident that Geraint wouldn't consider leaving Alwena so he was prepared to keep a very close watch on the girl, believing she would eventually lead him to his chief's wayward nephew.

Geraint had a real struggle with that cumbersome cart. He'd kept rigidly to the river bank until he found a suitable entry into the adjoining wood to conceal himself from the still marauding Romans. He had a clear view of the curve of the river and would be able to see when Alwena approached as he waited patiently for her there.

Tyddyn followed Alwena as she limped painfully along the twisting bends of the river bank.

Expecting Geraint to have been hugging the course of the river, her sharp eyes noted every little aspect along the way. There was no doubt in Tyddyn's mind that they would be heading for Deva as quickly as possible. He was interested to know how they'd attempt to gain access and whether they could be held there for Mawddach, so he made off to inform his chief without further delay.

When Alwena eventually caught up with Geraint, they continued with all the haste they could raise. The inclement weather they'd endured for most of the way had added greatly to their discomfort. They found it increasingly difficult to push the loaded cart through a series of deep pools of muddy water. Even with Alwena's limited help, the clumsy conveyance repeatedly slipped and swayed as if it had a mind of its own. Then, when they came to a particularly thick patch of sticky mud, it became firmly bogged down. All their combined heaving, pushing and pulling had no effect however how hard they tried. They simply couldn't move the vehicle which became trapped in that dense treacly bog. The more they struggled, the worse it seemed to become and when Geraint heard approaching voices yet again he hustled Alwena into the thickest part of a nearby wood. He hurriedly tore down a very leafy branch, re-emerged, and was placing it before the wheel to obtain purchase when the brutal Lucius came into view again.

"You've not made much progress, have you?" he scoffed and his accompanying escort laughed as Geraint unsuccessfully strained at the cart again. "I wouldn't be in your skin if you don't get that load of hay where it's needed pretty quickly," he added. "You could find yourself entertaining us on the day of the Big Feast along with that other horrible Celt we've already got – you could be an additional attraction!" The warning was not to be ignored but Geraint was wishing them anywhere before they discovered Alwena.

After they'd moved off again, Geraint waited a while then quietly called Alwena to come out. Together they strewed more leaf-covered branches under the wheels of the cart to assist it get a better grip on that slimy surface. It took the maximum energy of both and with feet slithering in clammy mud they eventually achieved a slight movement which was encouraging.

"Keep it going," panted Geraint in desperation knowing it was their only chance for if they stopped then there would be little likelihood of them ever moving the cart again. It had been tremendously hard going all the way, and Geraint was aware of how Alwena had struggled so hard to help him. He'd been extremely grateful for her assistance despite it being limited. He acknowledged she'd been a definite help when he realised he couldn't have managed on his own. On several other occasions, they got stuck in mud again and it had taken all their combined efforts to continue but they finally succeeded and continued to progress, though slowly.

Spotting in the distance what could only have been the outskirts of the fortress, Geraint assisted Alwena into the cart and covered her with hay. He would greatly miss her support for she'd been helpful, if in a limited way, by adding her weight to push that obstinate cart through the various muddy patches which they'd encountered. Even if he met no further opposition he realised it would be difficult enough for him to persuade the guards that he was genuine, but if Alwena had been beside him it would have been impossible to convince them of their innocence.

On the way to Deva there had been several other heavy deluges and he noticed that the river was starting to lap higher up the bank on both sides, and the tide seemed to be approaching its height by the time he arrived at the ford leading to the fortress. He anxiously watched as the water flowed swiftly over the small weir. The extra weight of Alwena was an added strain on both his arms and legs and his back ached dreadfully as he tried to cross the ford. He was amazed at the power of the water and wondered if he'd manage to cross. The conditions were far worse than he'd expected but being totally committed there was now no way back, for the guards could easily have noticed his presence and become suspicious.

He had great difficulty in manoeuvring the cart on his own as the water was almost up to his knees. He had to persevere or risk the consequences for the flow of water was trying to force him to the left, making the attempted crossing nightmarish. The uneven bed of the ford caused the cart to buck and sway dramatically with every step he took. It needed every ounce of his strength to hold it on course. He felt an increasing sympathy for Alwena who was having to take such a severe buffeting without knowing the reason. Even so, it was probably the extra weight stabilising the cart that had saved them both from being forced over the edge.

Twm certainly hadn't misled him when he'd described how the guards protecting the outer fortress had so cruelly ridiculed him. "What's happened to that idiot Twm who usually comes?" asked one when he eventually arrived at the gate.

"Weather's been too bad for that miserable weedy Celt to come out, I suppose," stated the other with heavy sarcasm.

"What a pity," responded his colleague with equal scorn. "I always look forward to having fun with that one." He turned to Geraint. "Still, you'll have to do now instead."

"They're probably saving that Twm for the gladiatorial demonstration in the Amphitheatre on the big Feast Day," added the first guard. "What a sight that would be. Wouldn't it be fun to see the old miser wrestle with a bundle of hay?" He seemed to reflect for a moment. "Perhaps it wouldn't be that funny after all though – the scraggy old devil would probably lose." His colleague stood laughing at Geraint's impatient embarrassment, not realising it was caused by his concern that each minute of delay risked the discovery of Alwena.

"Leave the lad alone," said the second guard mockingly. "He's only a youngster as you can see and he must have had enough trouble with that old Twm already. Anyway," he added, drawing his sword, "we'll soon see what this is all about." As he spoke, his sword came down towards the cart as if to slice the entire load in two. Geraint held his breath anticipating Alwena's scream but mercifully for him the sword was checked immediately it touched the load. "Ha, ha!" yelled the guard pointing to Geraint. "Just look at his face!"

"That's not the way to do it," stated his colleague. "I've always told you, if you're going to do a job then do it properly." With a determined look, he withdrew his sword and boasted, "Now I'll show you how to do it properly." Pulling his sword-arm back as far as he could, with the blade parallel to the ground, he drove it viciously towards the hay. Geraint was even more horrified. Alwena wouldn't only be discovered, but painfully killed. However, at the very last second, he too checked his movement and the blade barely touched the hay. Twisting his wrist with a wicked sneer, he smartly sheathed the blade again. "Ha, ha, ha," he guffawed even more loudly as he studied Geraint's pained expression. "This one's even more fun than that old Twm himself. You could see that he was terrified that I was going to scatter all his hay and he'd not get paid. I would have done too if it hadn't meant we'd have to clear it up." He paused. "It will certainly suit me if the old man doesn't come; there's even more fun with this one."

"By the look on his face he really thought you were going to chop up his precious load, didn't he?" said his companion. "Worried you wouldn't get paid if Brutus thought you'd brought him a load of rubbishy chaff, weren't you? Mind you, lucky you'll be if anything you get out of him anyway. A mean old mood he's been in for days and nobody's been able to please him."

They were both laughing loudly at his expense as they let him go but Geraint didn't care. He was sufficiently thankful to have eventually got through.

XXIII

Geraint found his way to the mansio without difficulty. As he entered the square he was puzzled to find a strange looking female staring hard at him. She had weird, straggly, cropped black hair and seemed to keep her peculiar eyes glued on him. He couldn't really understand it, yet there was the vaguest suggestion of a resemblance to someone he'd seen somewhere before. Her odd attitude worried him and he was disturbed at being unable to connect her with anyone. She was anything but attractive, but fixed an unwavering stare on him. She was coarsely dressed, repulsive looking and disfigured. Her eyes bored into him from her wounded face. "Whatever are you doing here?" she asked in a slurred almost unintelligible whisper through swollen lips. "You're a proper fool to have risked it. Don't you realise it's dangerous for you to be here." He stared uncomprehendingly. "Don't you know who I am? Can't you rec-og-nise me? See what they've done to me?" She was completely demented. Her voice was so husky he could barely make out her words. He continued to stare, realising that there was an indefinable familiarity about that strangely distorted voice. He studied her for some time and after a prolonged closer examination realisation slowly dawned.

He finally identified her as Marcia and couldn't believe the change in her. She'd obviously suffered greatly in such a short time. The raw scab-encrusted cheeks, the puffy eyes, non-existent eyebrows and eyelashes had made her appearance grotesque. It was no wonder he'd had difficulty in recognising her initially. It had all been the result of inhuman branding with hot irons that her diabolical father had insisted be carried out.

Geraint was uncertain of her intentions and was naturally so concerned that he treated her with great caution. "Whoever did that to you?" he enquired as tenderly as possible.

"Tha – t pig of a fath – er, and one day I'll kill him for it!" she stated viciously. Geraint couldn't believe that even the bestial Flavius could have stooped so low – and to disfigure his own daughter like that revealed the unimaginable cruelty of the man. He had now surpassed anything even Geraint could have expected of him. "What-ever are you do-ing here?" she asked again. Her speech was so slow and deliberate that he had great difficulty in understanding her. "You cou-ld be in ver-y gre-at dang-er and you can see it's too la-te to sa-ve me now." Geraint realised that she believed he'd been trailing her.

She clearly hoped that had been his intention. "Sti-ll I'm gla-d you've come. I of-ten won-der-ed if I'd ever see you again." The significance of her assumption wasn't wasted on him, and he was determined to store such comments for any possible future advantage. She was the only person there who could ever be of any help to them and he certainly wouldn't hesitate to use her if necessary. "I'm glad you ca-me," she repeated, "bu-t I did-n't wa-nt you to see me in th-is sta-te. How did you man-age to get past the gua-rds though?"

"Twm the Hayman isn't well and I had the chance to bring this hay in for him," he offered in a subdued voice. He watched her attempt a painfully wry smile. He wasn't prepared to take her into his confidence so he avoided any reference to Iorwerth.

Alwena, still crouching uncomfortably under the hay, was puzzled. Struggle as she might she couldn't identify the owner of that husky strangled voice. She couldn't understand who he was talking to or why he seemed to be wasting so much time. She was annoyed at the delay while she remained cooped up but hoped there was a good reason for it.

"So, you man-aged to get to De-va after all I see." He thought that a most ironic statement considering the condition of her eyes. "I'd ho-ped you wou-ld but you're too la-te for me now," she stated again in a tone which had a distinct note of regret. "Any-way you would-n't wa-nt me in this sta-te would you?" She remembered sadly, with a mixture of satisfaction and regret, the strong yet gentle way he'd held her for those few wonderful seconds at the copper mine when her father had struck her. She'd often longed for those brief seconds to be repeated and possibly extended.

"What are you doing here now, though?" he asked.

She bowed her head in shame and indicated her disfigurement. "Just look at me! I've been red-uc-ed to clea-ning out all the smel-ly old stables and doing ever-y dir-ty job they can find." Although her voice was still unclear her tone suddenly changed. "Don't let any-one know you recog-nise me or they'll be-come sus-pic-ious of you. If they see us tal-king like this, you cou-ld be in grave dan-ger." She suddenly took on an unexpected brusqueness. "Do-n't you dare daw-dle here like this! I'll show you where to de-posit the hay but be qui-ck about it!" She tipped him a sly jerk of the head, and following her direction, he noticed a legionnaire was suddenly approaching some distance away.

"That's the way to treat them you scruffy damned girl! Don't let those blasted unwelcome Celts linger! They see too much already! When you've done with him bring me some wine, you ugly looking wench!" Thankfully he crossed the yard to the building on the other side.

Inside the hay shed Geraint quietly asked why

they'd done that to her.

"It's what that inhum-an fa-ther of mine had me red-uced to," she stated in a venomous whisper as she stood beside the cart. "It's pun-ish-ment for let-ting you esca-pe. He swears I'll be work-ing here un-til my dy-ing day and he'll per-son-ally see that I'm never held in res-pect by any-one again."

Geraint felt that her speech was improving slightly, or perhaps he could have been getting more used to it. "Fa-ther says he'll encour-age every-one to point fingers at me and mock me." She drew a deep breath and spat contemptuously. "Oh, I hate him so much!" She paused and her voice took on an additional tone of bitterness. "I never thought I'd ever hate any-body like this."

An irate bellow shattered their few minutes together. "Where's that wine I told you to get me, you stupid looking wench?"

Geraint felt sorry for her.

"Listen to that! It's what I get from everybody all day and every day." He seemed to be hearing her more easily now and she appeared to have paused hopefully. "Don't forget I've got that room I told you about if you ever need it," she hurriedly whispered as she left. "I'll come back and make sure your unloaded cart is hidden as soon as I've got rid of this pest."

She left speedily to fulfil the legionnaire's demand and Alwena was more than relieved to be extricated from the stuffy hay which had practically suffocated her. She spent some time spitting out the chaff and seeds that had collected in her mouth.

"A surprise to find her it is!" Alwena spoke with an annoyed note of envy at having finally realised who Geraint had been talking with. "Out of place for her, doing such a dirty job as that after what she's been used to."

"Revoltingly disfigured she is too. Difficulty in recognising her I had," announced Geraint. "People stare at her wherever she goes. Tremendously ugly she is now. Even more inhumane than I ever thought, her father must be. How anyone could inflict such dreadful punishment on his own child is unbelievable. It shows what a real beast that wicked centurion is." The image of his father's killing had returned most vividly and with it his anger had increased. "Still it could possibly work to our advantage now," he said hopefully. "Perhaps she could help me to achieve my ambition to exterminate the beast if we play her right – and maybe she could also find out something useful about Iorwerth."

XXIV

When Marcia hurried back excitedly to Geraint, she was far from pleased to see Alwena there too. Yet the expression of hatred on Flavius' daughter's distorted face went unnoticed. Although not unduly surprised to find Alwena was a female, this altered her feelings for Geraint. Attempting to remove all signs of displeasure from her wretched face, she quickly changed her attitude and tried to appear friendly. She claimed that she could easily get Alwena a job in the baths, since she already had a limited experience of that work, and that would safeguard her position. Alwena readily agreed. She expected the minimum risk of detention once she got herself established as part of the system.

"I'll take you over there now and when you come back you'll both be able to sleep in the gap behind that boarding." She pointed to the hiding place she'd previously suggested to Geraint. It may be a bit of a squeeze for two of you but at least you'll be moderately safe. Although my father's out for your blood, fortunately he's not often around here. Anyway, he knows nothing of my secret room which you'll both be able to use in an emergency." She sighed despondently again. "I'll never forgive him, or forget the horrendous things he's had done to me. I'm longing to see his downfall and can't wait for it to happen. If ever I get the chance, I'll see it's absolute," she added forcibly.

They both felt able to trust her and gratefully accepted her suggestion in the hope that once they discovered Iorwerth's whereabouts they could achieve their desire.

A little time later, Marcia hurriedly returned to Geraint looking very concerned. "There's an extremely suspicious-looking, thin man making enquiries about a youth and a girl who are wanted by Flavius," she told them, in a voice which Geraint could now understand much more easily. "He had a nasty-looking weasel face and swore he saw you enter this area, so a search party is now on its way to investigate." She turned to Geraint. "Get into that gap, quick!" she directed. She grabbed Alwena's arm. "You'd better come with me. Hurry and I'll get you into the baths where you can start work without delay. There you'll avoid all suspicion; they'll soon consider you to be a legitimate part of the workforce."

Alwena welcomed the idea. It was her only means of getting inside the actual fortress. She hoped it would enable her to explore other parts of the complex and possibly get some indication of where they were holding Iorwerth.

As they left, Geraint secreted himself in the narrow gap behind the boarding and covered himself with some smelly straw. It was such an uncomfortably tight fit lying on his side that he wondered how he could have managed with Alwena there as well. Immediately he regretted having been in such a hurry to conceal himself as cramp was attacking him and the vile smell was overpowering. However, with the search party's voices already within earshot it was far too late to attempt to adjust his position.

The searchers covered the whole area without success but had overlooked Geraint's hideout. "What's behind that boarding?" asked one of them. Geraint wondered if the perspiration dripping from his brow onto the wet straw, which seemed to him to be flowing in an ear-splitting torrent, had given him away. He held his breath, as each spot of moisture dropping in the confined space seemed to resound throughout the entire area.

"Oh, it's only a pile of smelly straw," answered one. Geraint knew he was right; he could hardly breathe because of the stench. "If you want to see what's under it you can pull it out yourself because I'm not handling it. It's probably disease ridden by now anyway, so why bother to waste our time with it? There's not enough room for a dwarf to hide in there never mind the couple we're after. The space is too small for that supposedly big lad." He paused thoughtfully. "By the way who was that thin man who informed us about all this? Was he trying to mislead us?"

Geraint slowly and silently exhaled with relief, trusting that they wouldn't pursue matters further. Now it had been confirmed that Tyddyn was around he wondered what knavish tricks the despicable Ordovice would be up to next. Eventually, he was grateful to hear the searching party's receding steps and he hoped they'd all gone. Being unprepared to take unnecessary risks he waited painfully for a considerable time before he moved. The legionnaires had confirmed the fact that Tyddyn Fach was in the vicinity and Geraint wondered however he got there and whether the snivelling, interfering little rat could eventually disrupt their plans. He was convinced that Mawddach would be with him and it surprised him that the chief's privileges had extended that far. He realised that, if his uncle and that contemptible little character could use the fortress so easily, they would now have to be far more vigilant. Both Alwena and his safety depended on knowing whether they had those additional enemies to avoid while they were inside Deva.

CHAPTER

XXV

Marcia was treated with suspicion when she tried to pass Alwena through the South Gate. The sentries, who'd been instructed to refuse the disfigured female any entry, challenged her. "Exactly where do you think you're going?" demanded one who instantly confronted Marcia.

"I've got to take this horrible Celt to the baths; she's been detailed to work there."

"Then she'll have to go on her own. We've been directed not to let you enter."

Marcia was facing a problem. "You'll refuse me at your peril, legionnaire," she threatened boldly. "Flavius himself has personally ordered me to deliver this character…" She spat out the word with disgust, but her spite was missed by Alwena who'd been amazed at her boldness, "…to the baths myself in case she tries to escape. There have been complaints from the officers regarding the lack of hygiene and she's been instructed to have them cleaned and tidied ready for Feast Day. There'll be trouble for everyone if it's not done. Don't worry about me though for I won't be staying. The moment I've delivered her I'm to come back. I've been directed to tell you that if I'm not back in ten minutes you are to arrest me. As you can see, I've already had far too much punishment so you can rely on me arriving back in good time."

Alwena almost gave the game away. She was momentarily stopped in her tracks, feeling sure she'd seen the figure of Tyddyn Fach sidle furtively down a nearby alleyway. Thankfully he hadn't spotted her.

Marcia's firm stand convinced the guards to allow Alwena's passage. Both were let through and the young Celt was led to the baths. "Make yourself busy cleaning," she advised and was about to leave when Alwena, who was anxious asked, "A pass I'll need to get back past the guards, though won't I?" She simply had to get back to Geraint as quickly as she could and tell him about Tyddyn Fach. She also felt vulnerable and isolated without her younger friend.

"That won't be a problem," she lied. "They don't check people going out of the gate. They won't check me so you'll have no worry about that either." She made a hurried departure and was wearing an expression as near to a mischievous smile on her disfigured face as she could, but Alwena hadn't recognised it.

Alwena found that there was little to do and wondered why Marcia had taken her there in the first place. The baths were spotlessly clean and presentable so she hoped Flavius' daughter had known what she was doing. Regardless, she realised that she couldn't return too soon without the risk of raising suspicions so she set about pretending to work. To calm her increasing fears, she was humming a few old Celtic tunes which had been handed down for generations.

An officer came in for a bathe and hearing her quiet melody was very impressed. "We seem to have made one of these perishing natives happy," he muttered sarcastically to himself. "What a pity the rest of the rebellious lot cause us so much trouble."

Alwena was annoyed at his comment for she wasn't feeling at all happy and the effort of trying to appear composed was a tremendous strain. Still, she was glad she appeared to have allayed any suspicions he may have had. To prevent any possible questions from him she casually strolled out of the baths complex with a broom in her hand, and as she was being careful not to make herself too obvious she continued to hum a well-known Celtic melody as she slowly and methodically pretended to tidy the surrounds. Moving a little further on, she paused with surprise. A voice, almost as subdued as her own, had taken up the refrain and was very quietly singing the words of 'Mona – Mam Cymru'. It was the same tune that she'd been absent-mindedly humming. Her heart jumped with excitement. She realised that if she hadn't paused for breath she would probably have missed the connection.

"Iorwerth, it is?" she asked in an almost inaudible whisper.

"Yes, but who are you? Sound Celt you do." The question was equally muted.

"Alwena, I am. Followed Geraint I did, but back you sent me."

"Whatever do you think you're doing here, you young fool? Don't you realise you're in extreme danger?"

"Come with Geraint I have, to rescue you."

"What? Geraint as well is it? You've got no chance of ever getting me out of here and you'll be lucky if ever you get away too!"

"To rescue you before it's too late, we want."

"Where is Geraint then?"

"Hiding in the mansio. Waiting for me to go back there to him, he is."

"Ridiculous that is. No chance at all you've got. Their Feast Day is tomorrow and too well guarded I am. They want to torment me publicly in front of a massive crowd before sacrificing me. Fool I was; I shouldn't have been caught."

"If we can help, no harm to you will come."

"You'll never be able to stop them."

She was distraught, for she'd never expected Iorwerth to have been so resigned to his fate. She drew a deep breath in alarm and lowered her voice even more. "Coming someone is. Go now I must. I'll come back if I can," she promised as she hastily moved off.

"Hey you! What do you think you're doing out here?" It was the officer she'd left at the baths.

"This area wanted cleaning, see. Not dirty for the Festival it must be they said, so tidying it up I was."

"Just get back to where you belong! You're not supposed to be out here!" he screamed. "The cleaning of this area is none of your business. The baths are where you're to work, not here! You'd better get there quickly or I'll have you flogged."

Alwena's nerves tingled with a mixture of fear and excitement. Having found where Iorwerth was, she didn't want to spoil any chance of helping him and was relieved to have got off so lightly. She promised herself that she'd be more careful in future for it was vital that she transmitted the information regarding Iorwerth's whereabouts to Geraint as quickly as possible. She was even more anxious to return to him and despite glowing with excitement, she tried to remain as composed as possible when she presented herself at the South Gate. On arriving there she found she had a very serious problem.

"Who are you," demanded the officious legionnaire at the Gatehouse, "and where's your pass?" His colleague looked on in amusement.

"Not a pass I've got," she replied truthfully. "To work in the baths, brought here by Marcia I was. Not need a pass to go out I did, she said."

"Marcia? Who's Marcia?"

"Centurion Flavius' daughter she is."

"What! That ugly looking character that's been so severely punished? She's not even allowed to approach this Gate!"

"Brought me to work in the baths she did. Special permission she had. Not a pass needed for me to return she said," she repeated hopefully.

"Well, you do need a pass to get back to where you came from or you'll find yourself in real trouble." She was unsure of her position, yet felt somewhat relieved that the guard hadn't been over severe. She became confused, wondered why Marcia had told her there'd be no problem in returning. Slowly and despondently she retraced her steps, wondering where she could spend the night and what would become of her. She remembered a secluded corner of the baths and wondered if she could hide herself there and remain unobserved until she could find a way out and reach Geraint.

When Marcia returned to Geraint she found him quite worried.

"Will Alwena be all right in the baths?" he asked with obvious concern.

"Yes, perfectly all right. Nobody is at all likely to disturb her there and she'll certainly get into no trouble provided she keeps out of the way." The smile on her face was not evident because of its terrible distortion but her speech seemed less indistinct.

Geraint felt relieved. He'd suddenly started to appreciate that Alwena meant more to him than he'd realised and he knew he would never forgive himself if anything happened to her.

Marcia had been as good as her word in as much as the cart had been well concealed as she'd promised. Nobody would be able to find it without her help.

CHAPTER
XXVI

Alwena had a very uncomfortable night. Her thoughts floated from Tyddyn Fach, Iorwerth, Marcia, Mawddach to Flavius in rapid succession, then finally settled on Geraint. Tossing and turning in complete turmoil she imagined herself chasing the others to protect Geraint and perspiration poured off her in the process.

At first light, she was terrified to hear loud voices approaching. Frightened of being discovered, she remained stock still and strained to hear what was being said. To her surprise and utter disbelief she realised they were speaking in her own native tongue. They were obviously complaining in subdued Celtic tones and her hopes instantly soared. Creeping nearer to them she learned that they were grumbling at being forced to clean the entire outside of the building ready for the great Feast Day celebration. She soon learned that they were part of a very sizable party of cleaners, the others having been sent to different parts of the fortress.

Armed with such knowledge and believing their unobtrusive rebellious attitude could be an advantage she boldly revealed herself. "Fellow Cymru's you are then?" she queried with confidence as she presented herself to them. "Ordovice or Deceangli then you are, like?"

"Deceangli me, and Megan here Ordovice is," said the more buxom of the two as she pointed to her companion. Alwena was delighted to see two from opposing tribes getting along in such a peaceful and friendly manner. Obviously they both hated the Romans so much that they'd become sociable and she only hoped that both tribes could find a means to join in a similar way.

"Alwena, I am. Ordovice too, see," she offered proudly, delighted that one belonged to her own tribe. "Important news about Iorwerth Morgwn I have too!"

"What then is that news?" enquired Megan with undisguised interest.

"A prisoner not far from here, he is."

"Where is that then?"

"Just down there on the other side of that wall he is, see." She indicated the general direction. "I want to get out to tell my friend but no pass to get out I've got."

"However did you get in then?" enquired Megan mystified.

Alwena explained. "I was brought here from the mansio and was told no pass I'd need to get out, but without one not past those damned guards can I get!"

"No trouble getting you out it will be," promised the Deceangli. "Many of us came in and one more going out won't be noticed. Yesterday a young boy got through and not noticed he was. Looking for a young man and a girl he said."

Alwena became apprehensive, wondered if it really could have been Arwyn and became worried that his intention could have been to expose them. He'd stated several times previously that he'd been taught not to trust the Ordovices. Casting the thought from her mind, she concentrated more on the prospect of having found a possible way out. "How did you get him through the guards then?" she asked.

"A real puzzle that is. In the middle of us he was. A guard thought he'd seen him, but not to be seen the boy was when we were searched. Completely disappeared he had and not know where to or how, we do."

As they formed up at the South Gate one of the sentries was instantly suspicious. "There's one more going back than came in," he stated with confidence and when Alwena heard him, her heart sank. Holding her breath nervously she wondered whether this second attempt was going to fail as badly as the first.

"You sure?" questioned his colleague doubtfully.

"Course I am sure! Know how to count don't I?"

"Not so sure about that. Not bad when you're sober but since you had an abundance of that horrible vino again last night it's probably dulled your senses. You really should drink less you know!"

"Nonsense, I can take much more wine than that and still count properly," he offered somewhat smugly.

"Well you certainly couldn't count the number of gladiators in the arena last Feast Day – and that was certainly due to the amount of wine you'd had!"

"That wasn't the wine. It was such a hot day for a change – something we'd not had since coming to this stupid country- that the heat upset me. I wasn't used to it being that hot over here," he repeated.

Alwena became increasingly nervous as their banter went on. They were so near the gateway she could almost have put her hand through to the other side. Desperation took over. She was so tantalisingly near achieving her objective yet appeared to be failing once again. Mere yards away from release, she frantically willed herself to be on the far side of the gateway. The few minutes they'd been held up had seemed like an age before she heard the other guard object to his colleague's suggestion for a second count.

"We just can't afford to keep this lot hanging about here again like we did yesterday simply because you can't count properly," he scolded. "We'll soon have that blasted centurion coming over again to reprimand us if we hold them up much longer. We'd better let them through before he notices that we've caused a delay again."

"It's your responsibility if things go wrong then. I still tell you there is one too many!"

"Just stop talking such rubbish and let them go through. I tell you again, you should stop drinking so much wine, it's doing you no good."

Alwena was pleased that the guards were different from the very officious two who'd denied her entry the previous day. She realised that she wouldn't have been so lucky with them, and once they were through the South Gate she issued an immense sigh of relief. The group turned left and although it didn't suit Alwena she was forced to accept it. With the mansio in the opposite direction it put her in quite a quandary. To have hived herself off and gone to the right on her own would have alerted the sentries they'd just passed through and that would have created a mountain of unwanted trouble. Instead, despite her misgivings she was forced to stay with them until they reached the canabae and, as they were about to leave, they got caught up in a torchlight horde taking Iorwerth to his overnight cell, though she hadn't realised who it was.

Not wishing to become involved any more, she separated herself from the other women and hid in a recessed doorway until things got quieter. As the noise was subsiding she was shocked to see Arwyn come out of the shadows to her left.

"Managed to get out then, did you?" She couldn't decide whether he was pleased or annoyed. His whispered tone had given no indication, and as soon as the crowd was out of sight she told Arwyn to leave her. Unbeknown to both, Geraint himself was only two blocks away. Stealthily she made her way back towards the mansio hoping to find Mawddach's nephew there.

The search party was still operating and she had to hide constantly to avoid them. Having had several near misses, she decided it was too risky to aim for the mansio and she was about to make her way towards Marcia's room when she found the route blocked again by the same chanting crowd. She squeezed herself into a tiny niche to avoid detection and stayed there for some time. Just as she thought the way was clear enough for her to move she froze. A hand grabbed her arm, she gasped and was about to scream when a whispered young voice stopped her. "Don't shout!" it warned urgently, "and all right you'll be."

CHAPTER

XXVII

M arcia deliberately tormented Geraint. She stated that Alwena had probably already discovered Iorwerth who was securely held within the walls near to where she was working.

"They're going to bait him in the Amphitheatre at tomorrow's Feast Day. He'll be the main attraction and will be attacked and tortured for as long as possible to satisfy everyone watching," she offered. "He'll receive hours of excruciating pain at the hands of the most villainous legionnaires before he'll be sacrificed by my cowardly father, who has claimed the privilege of delivering the final thrusts when Iowerth is drawing his last gasps. My father, in spite of his dreadful reputation, will be too conceited to tackle him before he's completely weakened. He wouldn't like to prolong the fatal blow before so many people, as that would show him up and the standing which he so enjoys would be greatly reduced." She didn't show the slightest sign of affection for her father now. "There's no way he'd risk such a disgrace."

"Could it not be stopped in any way at all?" enquired Geraint with concern.

"No. The victim will be too well guarded tonight

to achieve that. He'll be brought to the Amphitheatre in a noisy torchlight procession a little later and housed there overnight, guarded by Gregorius who's renowned for his vigilance. He'll then be taken into the arena at the appropriate time ready for the display. Tomorrow will certainly be an extremely humiliating day for him. He'll be jeered at and spat upon by everyone present before finally being put to death." There wasn't the slightest indication of sympathy in her voice as she detailed the forthcoming event. It was almost as if she was eagerly looking forward to it all herself.

Geraint became more distraught: he couldn't stand the thought of Iorwerth, whom he'd always considered a great Celtic warrior, being so shamefully treated. "Is there no possible way we could rescue him at all?" he enquired again with increased distress.

"Not a chance. You'd have to get past the South Gate sentries – and you couldn't do that without a pass even if you were a well-known Roman. Even if you did possibly get through, with the entire fortress looking out for you there'd be no likelihood of you getting very far and you'd probably end up alongside Iorwerth in the arena. As you probably know, I am not allowed into the fortress myself any more since my damned father had this revolting thing done to me." The bitterness in her voice was total. She put her hand to her cheek and the tears started to form in her swollen eyes. "I swear he'll pay for this if it's the last thing I do."

Geraint stood deep in thought. His aim in getting to Deva had been to rescue Iorwerth and that now seemed a total impossibility.

At that very moment, they heard the crowd of Romans coming into the mansio and knew it was time for them to move.

"He must be somewhere here," a voice called out. "That weedy Celt with Mawddach said he'd seen him."

"Quick! This way!" whispered Marcia, leading him through a narrow gap in the mansio while the searchers were still sufficiently far off. They emerged on the west side of the South Gate. "If we skirt the walls right round to the other side we should be able to reach my room unseen," Marcia stated cautiously. "It won't take long but we'll have to be very careful."

As they were approaching the West Gate, Marcia moved him out towards the harbour to sneak between the two large warehouses which stored lead and silver from the Celtic mines. On nearing the far end of the sheds, Geraint suddenly came face to face with Tyddyn Fach and the puny little Ordovice drew a shocked breath and hurriedly turned to flee but Geraint was too quick. Ignoring the possibility of being discovered he left Marcia and raced after him. Coming up behind him, Geraint wrapped his arm around his neck and grabbed his throat. Holding him in a vice-like grip he shook him like the rat he resembled.

"If squeak you do, you scum, the last it will be," Geraint threatened and for the first time he noticed that Tyddyn was genuinely scared. The confidence of the weedy little informer appeared to have been completely drained. He'd always been confident in the knowledge of Mawddach's protection but now that his chief was not near him he was concerned. In his present situation, his normal bravado had totally deserted him.

Twisting the smaller man's arm until it really hurt, Geraint took him to a recess below the walls towards the northern side of the harbour to make sure that they were well out of view of the West Gate sentries. "You'd better talk now or I'll not hesitate to toss you into the harbour and make sure that you don't come up again."

"To know what, you want?"

"Where that despicable leader Mawddach is hiding."

"I do not know."

"Liar! Where to find him when tales you must tell, you always know. Remember quickly you'd better, as itching I am to see the splash when you hit that icy water." As he spoke he was already forcing Tyddyn towards the water's edge.

"No! No!" he squeaked almost inaudibly. "With Flavius, he is."

"Where?"

"The fortress they're within. Beneath the granaries, a room there is. Telling about arrangements when they move Iorwerth from the Amphitheatre he was. Kept there until ready for tomorrow's celebration, he'll be."

"Which room in the Amphitheatre will he be in?"

"Know – really I do not." He started to scream as Geraint twisted his arm with force.

"Stop that noise," he hissed. "If you alert the sentries I'll really make you suffer. Come with me now and quiet keep! If you notify anyone of our presence, you'll not be able to do anything again!"

Most in Deva were enjoying the build up to the following day's celebrations as Geraint stealthily led Tyddyn round the outside of the north end of the fortress. He made sure that they kept tightly to the wall and as they were making their way towards the North Gate he savagely thrust him against the wall and pinned his arm tightly against his throat to prevent him calling out. The action had caused Tyddyn an involuntary grunt and a sentry pacing restlessly outside the gate called out with a note of concern, "I'm sure I heard someone out there."

"No. It'll be all the noise coming from those lucky winebibbers who've already started their Feast

Day celebrations that you've heard," suggested his colleague with a strong note of envy.

"No. It definitely sounded as if someone was trying to sneak past."

"Rubbish. You've undoubtedly simply imagined things. You're probably like me, annoyed that you're not able to indulge yourself until this stint of duty is over. Just come over here and I'll show you what you've heard."

As the sentry returned through the gateway Geraint, with his hand firmly over his captive's mouth, forced him along the wall towards the gate. He saw a sentry some way inside the fortress pointing something out to his companion. They edged past unobserved and quietly rounded the north-east corner towards the parade. He was grateful that nobody was on the parapet above to spot them. His intention had been to take Tyddyn to Marcia's room but as they neared the East Gate the torchlight procession was emerging yet again, accompanied by a group of wine-soaked revellers.

Maddened at the sight of Iorwerth, already the recipient of much beating and abuse, Geraint was furious that he was not able to help him. With his hand over Tyddyn's mouth again he pinched his nostrils so that he could hardly breathe as he held the informer close to the wall until the procession had passed. When satisfied that it had gone, he followed at a discreet distance, hoping to see where they were taking his father's lieutenant. Thankfully, as the crowd passed the canabae – an area comprising houses, shops and taverns – many others joined the procession, which made him slightly safer as there would be few remaining to notice them.

There was a sudden unexpected pause in the procession which for some unaccountable reason had slowed to a halt. Geraint was relieved to discover that it hadn't been to frequent the taverns which could possibly have delayed matters even further. Obviously, they were going to enjoy such pleasure a little later, but the baiting of Iorwerth appeared to be far more important for them at that moment.

Concealing himself and Tyddyn in a shadowy alleyway he had a tremendous fright. A Roman soldier staggered out of a tavern and accosted them in a heavily slurred voice. He yelled, "Come and join the fun, won't yer friends?" Fortunately, he stumbled off without pursuing the matter and Geraint could breathe normally again. Surreptitiously following the raucous gathering as far as the Amphitheatre, they discovered the entrance that they'd taken Iorwerth through but were disappointed not to be able to identify where they were holding him. Still, having made a mental note of the gate he'd entered by, he hoped that that would prove useful.

XXVIII

Marcia was extremely annoyed with Geraint when he finally arrived at her room. "So, you've decided to come back after leaving me have you?" she bawled. "And what have you brought this snivelling character here for?" The glower she gave Tyddyn made him squirm. Despite her caustic greeting as she let them in, Geraint noticed the look of relief on the informer's face. The prying little Ordovice had already informed Flavius of Marcia's secret room.

As soon as they were inside, Geraint tied Tyddyn's hands and feet and hurled him into the corner to prevent their having to worry about him. He turned to Marcia. "What has become of Alwena?" he asked with a note of concern.

Marcia turned on him savagely. "Alwena! Alwena! Alwena! Always Alwena isn't it – and never Marcia! You think more of her and that rebellious countryman of yours than you ever do of me!"

Geraint, recognising that he was suddenly on slippery ground, realised he'd have to handle her very carefully. "Well about you a lot I think too," he lied, appreciating that he was still very much in need of her help if he was ever to be able to assist Iorwerth.

"I don't think you do," she snarled. "Just look at all this!" She pointed to her disfigurement again. I got all this through trying to help you! Does that not mean anything to you?"

"Yes. Yes, I appreciate you very much and regret what has happened to you, on behalf of Alwena and me!"

"Alwena! Alwena! Alwena once more, is it? Never Marcia at all I hear from you! Well, you'll be very lucky if ever you see her again."

Geraint was livid. He grabbed hold of her roughly and shook her. "Why? What have you done with her?"

"I've looked after her all right, like I said. She's inside the fortress and won't get out of there in hurry. Someone will discover exactly who she is now – and she'll have to take the consequences!"

"Why you…" His vindictiveness was stilled by a savage pounding on the door. Marcia went to open it.

"You!" she exclaimed incredulously as she faced Alwena who'd got there with the help of Arwyn. She'd been led through a maze of entries and buildings to avoid detection before he disappeared into thin air again as they reached Marcia's room.

"Yes, it's me, all right," responded Alwena pushing past the obstructing Marcia as she spotted Geraint.

It was surprising that the two hadn't bumped into

each other in the canabae for they'd been mere doors apart. Before Arwyn had discovered her, she'd been in the path of those escorting Iorwerth, trying to find a way to Marcia's. She'd taken refuge in a doorway which was just around the corner from Geraint's hideout. "Surprised to see me, aren't you? Get out of that fortress without a pass you said I could – but knew I couldn't."

Marcia's mutilated face became more distorted as it broke into a hideous sneer. She said nothing but the hateful expression spoke volumes.

Tyddyn, lying in the corner, smiled. He'd very quickly sensed he now had a lever to cause trouble between Marcia and the fugitives.

Unable to contain herself, Alwena exploded. "Spoken to Iorwerth I have."

"Not possible you did. A large mob taking him to the Amphitheatre we saw. Locked up for tomorrow's taunting all night he will be."

"Before they took him I spoke with him – very briefly."

"Where was that?" Geraint's doubt had increased.

"Forced to stay in the baths I was. Wandered outside humming 'Mona – Mam Cymru' to myself I did, when from the other side of a wall, singing the words he joined me. Told him trying to rescue him you were and impossible it was, he said."

"Then he knows I'm here, you say?"

"Yes."

"Well something about it I'd better try to do then. Don't want him to think I've let him down again." He moved towards the door.

"I'll hate you if you go! I'll never help you again!" Since Marcia seemed to be losing the person she'd sacrificed so much for, her loathing was unmistakable.

"Wait for me – I'm coming too!" called Alwena and the moment they went through the door Marcia released Tyddyn Fach.

"Make sure they get caught," she ordered venomously as he hurriedly massaged his wrists and ankles before following the youngsters. Tyddyn Fach wasted no time. Quickly following, he soon spotted them dashing ahead. He stalked them with his usual care and saw them heading for the east side of the Amphitheatre. Seeing them enter with caution, he realised their intention and rushed to inform Mawddach.

Meantime, Geraint was outlining his plan to Alwena. "Dark enough the Amphitheatre is tonight. To enter from here without being seen is quite possible. To find where they're holding Iorwerth and how to free him we might be able." They kept low, inconspicuously skirting the ring of seats as they made their way westward. With all the noisy revelry continuing, they were forced to hide between benches until the crowds departed. There was no possibility of doing anything positive with so many people around so they prepared themselves for a long wait.

Before Tyddyn Fach had been able to find Mawddach, Flavius had barged into Marcia's room in a furious state. Grabbing his daughter violently he smacked her distorted face. "What's all this about you hiding that villainous Celt you know I'm after?" he screamed as he hurled her to the floor.

"Leave me alone, you beast!" she howled from her prostrate position. "Haven't you done enough damage to me already?"

"What punishment you've already had, is nothing to what you'll get now!" he bellowed drawing out his dagger. "I'll see you're never able to disgrace me again!" His fury terrified her but before he could execute his dastardly deed the door burst open and Mawddach barged in followed by his sneaky informer.

"The Amphitheatre now they're in, Flavius. Catch them we will if hurry we do!" Flavius, holding the dagger above his daughter's head had been so startled by the disturbance that he'd turned. At the same time Marcia had instinctively twisted to the right and the blade had cut into her left shoulder with paralysing effect.

"Your punishment will be finalised when we've caught those two horrible young Celts and there'll be absolutely nowhere for you to hide from now on I promise you! You'll be hounded out and punished wherever you go – and I'll be back to do it!"

As Flavius left with Mawddach and his informant, Marcia gazed at her saturated garments and struggled to stem the blood flowing from her wounded shoulder. With a supreme effort, weak as she was, she followed her father with immense determination.

At that time, Geraint and Alwena had been gently edging their way towards the west side of the Amphitheatre when a legionnaire with a flaming torch, some twenty yards higher up, had his back to them. Geraint was pondering how to pass him when Alwena gave an involuntary sneeze.

The Roman turned and challenged. "Who are you, and what are you doing there?"

"Where you are, stay down Geraint," she whispered. "Away with this we'll get if lucky we are." She stood up and made her way towards the soldier. She forced herself to speak very slowly determined not to give away her Celtic background as she carefully rephrased her natural speech. "I wa-s try-ing to get to that horr-ible Celt you-'re hold-ing," she offered, as convincingly as she could.

I wan-t to stri-ke him for caus-ing so much trou-ble and won-der-ed if I could get at him this wa-y."

The legionnaire laughed. "Nobody will ever get anywhere near him tonight. He's being very carefully guarded by Gregorius. He'll be hauled out for the entertainment tomorrow and get his desert from those specially chosen. You'd better go back where you came from because you're wasting your time around here. You'll be able to see plenty of people striking him tomorrow so that should be enough for you."

"Wha- t a pi-ty!" Not waiting to pursue the matter further, she retraced her steps without arousing his suspicion. Taking care not to give Geraint away, she carefully strode past him and on turning back some distance away she noticed that the Roman had moved on and the entire area had been plunged back into darkness again.

XXIX

Tyddyn, full of confidence again, led Flavius and Mawddach to the east side of the Amphitheatre. Although they'd become accustomed to the gloom it was still too dark for them to see the youngsters. Flavius called out furiously. "Guard! Has a young Celt and a girl come this way?"

The guard rushed to his summons. "No. Only a girl trying to get to the prisoner. Wanted to strike him for what he'd done to her family; had found it impossible to reach him from the other side because of the crowd. Told her she was wasting her time and she went back where she came from."

"Fool!" snapped Flavius. "You've probably let a wanted enemy escape. You're under arrest! You'll be severely punished for this!" Crouching in the funereal blackness Geraint had heard every word and waited patiently until the three had escorted the guard from sight. He then followed Alwena towards the south side of the Amphitheatre where they found steps leading towards a narrow passage. He picked up a rounded stone as they carefully edged their way forward. The tunnel seemed to run all the way around the arena and they realised they'd have to move fast, at the same time exercising the strictest caution to avoid Flavius. A strident voice echoed impatiently down the corridor and they hoped it wasn't Flavius.

Suddenly the chamber was lit up by two legionnaires carrying lighted torches. They were approaching noisily and Geraint just had time to push Alwena into a nearby dark curved alcove and squeeze in beside her. "Looking for two young Celts," said one as they neared them. "Flavius is desperate for their capture. He thinks they might be trying to release the prisoner who was brought in tonight."

"Not much chance of that with Gregorius guarding him. Nobody ever gets past Gregorius you know!"

"Oh, yes! Safe enough in his hands he'll be. He's the best sentinel we've got but you know how Flavius reacts at a time like this."

Geraint's hopes were fading rapidly. He knew he needed some element of luck to free Iorwerth. Now it appeared he'd need more than just luck. When the Romans' footsteps had faded Geraint nervously looked out and, seeing nothing in the gloom, he quickly turned back. "Come on," he whispered, "risk it we've got to!" They followed the passageway contours, and negotiating a bend some fifty yards on they spotted the indistinct outline of a sentry outside a door. Withdrawing a few feet, Geraint skilfully hurled the stone past the armed Roman and it skidded from wall to wall for some distance beyond him. The sentinel checked that all was well before setting off to investigate. The timing had been perfect and the sentry's absence gave them the opportunity they sought. During his absence, Geraint and Alwena slipped into the cell and quickly indicated silence to Iorwerth. Alwena partly closed the door while Geraint severed the prisoner's bonds.

When the guard returned, he was amazed. He flung the door open to ensure Iorwerth was still there and received a shock. As he stepped inside Alwena slammed the door while Geraint and Iorwerth attacked the surprised Roman. They gagged him, bound his hands and feet and dragged him to the farthest corner of the unlighted cell.

Opening the door to make a dash for it, Geraint heard the unmistakable voice of Flavius accompanied by those of Mawddach and Tyddyn which caused him to curse. "Where's the guard for this prisoner?" Flavius screamed. "This man should never have been given the remotest chance to escape. He's far too dangerous to be left unattended. Has everyone in the Legion lost their senses?" He entered the cell with a drawn sword and Mawddach's immense frame filled the doorway to prevent any means of escape. Flavius was too irate to notice the bound sentry. "Ah! Three of you together!" His rage got the upper hand. "Well, I had far too much trouble with that slippery father of yours until I slew him and I've no intention of having similar trouble with you!" He slashed at him with his sword but Geraint skilfully sidestepped to avoid him and Iorwerth lunged at him. Flavius was an expert with the sword and having caught sight of the advance from the corner of his eye, his sword scratched Iorwerth and drew blood from his shoulder. At the same time Mawddach had grabbed his former tribesman and held him in a secure grip.

"Don't injure him too much Mawddach," instructed Flavius. "We want him in reasonable shape for tomorrow's fun." Iorwerth clutched his shoulder to stem the blood. Fortunately, it wasn't severe. "That cut is nothing to what you'll get tomorrow," he promised wickedly. "I'll be delighted to see the terror on your faces as I carve you up in pieces before the crowded auditorium, then deliver the final thrust."

"Watch out!" Tyddyn cried.

Marcia, still bleeding profusely, staggered into the cell clutching a dagger and before Flavius could move, gave one powerful and determined lunge with the dagger into his back before she collapsed on top of him. "That's for what you did to me, you beast!" she gasped almost inaudibly. "I would have done it years ago too, if I'd known you'd ever have treated me like this!" The effort had been too much for her and her body had sagged. She just gave a couple of small jerks and then lay motionless, unable to move again.

The dagger had been held so tightly that it had exited her father's falling body and then dropped from her lifeless hand.

Mawddach, with his massive arm wrapped tightly around Iorwerth's throat, took command and Iorwerth's eyes expressed his agony. "Send you after that brother of mine now I would! What you deserve that is! Seemed devoted to him you did, but sent him from this life for me the Romans did. You too they'll take tomorrow, but a mighty painful treat they'll want to give you first so I won't disappoint them. It will give me pleasure to see you humiliated before so many people." He turned to address Tyddyn. "On those two keep your eye. If any move they make, call me and not for tomorrow's performance I'll wait. Finish these traitors myself I will then!"

CHAPTER
XXX

As Flavius lay breathless and wounded on the cell floor he heard a groan from the darkened corner. It was the sentinel and he gaspingly cursed the man for his inefficiency. With a stupendous effort, he picked up the dagger and crawled to the soldier's assistance. "You'll certainly suffer for this," he snarled weakly but the effort had completely drained him. By sheer determination he managed to sever the bond on the captive's wrists and the sentry quickly removed the gag and freed his feet.

"There was something…" he started to explain.

"…No excuses," snapped Flavius as firmly as he could, mustering all his available energy even in his fragile state: his brutality was still evident despite his weakness. "Get after them if you value your life," he gasped.

The subordinate wasted no time. Flavius' authority was still supreme as far as he was concerned. He was heading towards the door on wobbly legs before the centurion had had time to draw a second breath.

"Stop those people," he shouted trusting someone would hear him. His raucous echo reverberated along the curving unlighted corridor, fading in volume as it went. But none of that had any effect on Geraint whose reaction was even quicker than that of the sentinel and he tripped him up. The Roman barged into Mawddach whose hold on Iorwerth was weakened.

"Soon someone come to help me," pleaded Mawddach, finding it difficult to keep hold of Iorwerth and protect himself, as Geraint and Alwena having evaded the now prostrate centurion, had also attacked him. Hywel's son had no intention of attempting to escape unless he could ensure Iorwerth was safe. He resolved that any chance of getting away they'd all have to take together for he certainly hadn't gone all that far to desert his father's friend at that stage. Totally convinced now that his cruel uncle had pandered to the Romans so treacherously and for so long, the nephew renewed his vow to settle that score on his father's behalf.

Geraint held his breath as he caught sight of three legionnaires running towards the cell with a lighted torch, and events moved quickly. Miraculously and unexpectedly there was a growl. Mawddach's hound sprang at the legionnaire holding the torch, to protect his friend. The legionnaire slackened his grip and, as the light was falling, Geraint wasted no time. He quickly grabbed it and wielded in the faces of the other two. They were unable to draw their swords in such a confined space and were stopped in their tracks.

"Down!" screamed Mawddach at the dog as he

attempted to kick it. He missed, and with bared teeth the animal lurched at his master with such force as to knock him over and locked its fangs so tightly round Mawddach's throat that he could neither move nor speak. He issued a horrible gurgling sound as blood flowed in bursts over the dog that was still gripping his throat. "Deserved that for many years you have," stated Geraint. He then noticed one of the Romans draw a dagger, but before he could move the adversary threw up his arms and fell forward with a knife in his back.

Little Arwyn quickly extracted the blade and with an almost continuous movement stabbed the remaining soldier as he moved forward. "Come on! Out quick we've got to go!" yelled the young Deceangli as Geraint took a hasty look at Mawddach to confirm that the hound had completed its work. He also looked for Tyddyn but there was no sign of that horrible little troublemaker. He seemed to have completely disappeared yet again.

"The way we came, we'd better go," he instructed. "Follow the boy. Know what to do he will. Plunge into the river and make upstream as fast as you can. They'll expect us to be carried to the weir so will cover that area. There's something I want to settle, then catch you up I will." At that moment, the freed sentinel who'd grabbed Flavius' weapon blocked his way with a drawn sword. The hound hurled itself at him but had no chance of survival. The weapon was thrust into the animal and Arwyn again came to the rescue. Before the guard could withdraw his sword, the youngster had hurled a stone with such accuracy that it had hit him in the face. "Come on!" he yelled again grabbing Geraint's arm with increased urgency. "We'll have the whole garrison on us if we don't move fast."

Iorwerth and Alwena had been reluctant to leave Geraint but he'd insisted so forcibly that they'd finally given in. As he was following Arwyn he glanced into the cell and picked out the prone body of Flavius.

"At last, revenge I've witnessed," he called coolly to himself as he went. "I would willingly have killed you myself but your daughter rightly denied me the privilege for what you did to her, you beast. However, there's no blood on my hands like there is on yours and you've certainly not been let off after all these years. Eight years-old only I was at the time, and to see you dead I promised myself then!"

He heard a commotion coming nearer and the glow of a lighted torch showed along the passageway to his left. As he turned to escape he caught sight of the lifeless dog. Its glassy eyes showed an expression of affection and Geraint felt a tear trickle down his cheek.

"Heading for the steps they entered by, it seems," a soldier called. "Trying to get to the river, I suppose."

"There they are! Let's get them!" called another. Geraint was grateful to Alwena who'd insisted that he learn to swim all those years ago, as he outstripped the pursuing Romans in their heavy armour. Even so Arwyn left him standing. The other two had hesitated at the riverside waiting to see if they needed help. "In the water, quick!" he snapped. "Move!" He hurled himself in after them along with Arwyn. They all fought desperately against the ebbing tide to avoid the weir, mostly under water. Several javelins were thrown at them and fortunately all missed.

Catching up with their companions some way up the river they all crawled on to the bank to regain their breath before continuing.

CHAPTER
XXXI

Geraint thanked the rascally Arwyn who'd been a complete mystery to him but his assistance had been invaluable. They made towards Holtinium as quickly as they could because Geraint owed Twm an apology for losing his cart.

"Not to bother you that is," stated Twm. "An old cart it was and no more hay to carry just now there is. Too old to struggle all that way again too, I am."

Geraint then turned his attention to getting back to the tribe and accepting the chieftainship in place of his uncle. He was convinced that he'd enjoy having that necessary twig affixed to the crow's mouth and he'd really respect it. He was determined to rule much more fairly than his predecessor, but wasn't sure what to do with the sneaky Tyddyn Fach for he knew he'd have to be very severe with him if he continued with his snooping and interfering ways. That problem was soon solved, when some time later he heard that the distrustful little Ordovice had slipped up and been captured by the Romans. That had resolved matters for him as he was their problem now. He had no intention of interfering; the rascal had brought it all on himself and the outcome was what he truly deserved.

He turned to Arwyn. "Well this is goodbye to you my young friend. Thank you for all your help and support. We certainly wouldn't have been able to free Iorwerth without you and I trust that this is not the end of our friendship. I hope to be seeing you again in the future, even though you are a Deceangli and I'm an Ordovice"

"There's no doubt you'll be seeing me for a long time because I'm not going anywhere. I'm coming with you and we'll go to see Berwyn Goch to resolve things between our two tribes now that the dreadful Mawddach Du has gone. You've often said that we're all Celts and should treat each other as such with peaceful respect, so now's the time to do it!"

Geraint was pleased at the boy's attitude and together they went to see the Deceangli leader. He was amazed at the reception young Arwyn received from his chief when he'd outlined what had happened and detailed how Geraint had been determined to rescue Iorwerth. Berwyn Goch had been grateful for Iorwerth's release because he'd become fond of him and trusted him. He was still more delighted with the suggestion of uniting the two tribes, which Geraint had proposed as firmly as his father had.

Although he'd failed in his vow to kill either Flavius or Mawddach, he was perfectly satisfied that both had been exterminated by other hands. Knowing that he'd now have Alwena permanently at his side, that

Iorwerth had become his most devoted friend, for which he was extremely grateful, and Berwyn Goch had completely given up any animosity towards the Ordovices he was satisfied.

Yet his most cherished delight lay in the belief that Hywel would be looking down on him with tremendous pride and gratitude for achieving his unfulfilled ambition, so many years after his own attempt, to unite the tribes.

The End